D1271959

LOVE IN LANCASTER COUNTY

SECRET MELODY

· Katy Lee ·

Annie's®

Books in the Love in Lancaster County series

Library of Congress-in-Publication Data
Secret Melody / by Katy Lee
p. cm.
I. Title
                    2021950323

AnniesFiction.com
(800) 282-6643
Love in Lancaster County™
Series Creator: Shari Lohner

10 11 12 13 14 | Printed in South Korea | 9 8 7 6 5 4 3 2 1

CHAPTER ONE

Following the rules was supposed to lead a person to success, or so Ruth Griffin had thought. But Ruth felt like anything but successful now. She hung her head low as she rode in her coworker Val's little hatchback toward the Grille. According to Val, getting fired called for a night out. All Ruth wanted to do was go home and mope. Her time at the Pittsburgh Savings and Loan had come to an abrupt end. Ruth had been fired—not for breaking a rule, but for refusing to break one.

"I'm so sorry this has happened to you. There's got to be something better for you out there." Val waved a hand at her windshield to implicate some job that would presumably appear in the world. "I always knew that Taylor was bad news. How dare he put you in this situation! I'm sure if we go to Mr. Williams and explain how his grandson has treated you, he'll reinstate you. Taylor wanted you to steal for him."

"I already told Mr. Williams all that. He didn't believe me. He thinks Taylor can do no wrong." Ruth sighed and dropped her head back against the headrest. "Kathy's going to be furious that I lost my job."

Ruth knew she sounded dramatic, but she was also sure that what she'd said was true. Her sister, who was ten years older than Ruth, had taken her in years before, after their parents were killed in a robbery. Since the day Ruth had arrived on her doorstep, Kathy had clearly resented having to raise her. Now Ruth was twenty-one, and she'd been working hard to save up for her own place. Her job at the bank was supposed to help her move toward that goal. "I'm not looking forward to facing her," Ruth admitted.

"That's why I'm taking you out. Wednesday night is karaoke night at the Grille."

"You mean a bunch of mediocre singers singing a bunch of old songs? I'll pass." Ruth would much rather get lost in a book than submit herself to a rowdy crowd. "I don't think this is a good idea. I won't be good company tonight. I've got a different kind of music to face at home anyway."

"I'm not taking no for an answer. And we're almost there." Val took the next exit off the highway. "You need to stop being afraid of your own shadow. Singing will be good for you."

Val talked the rest of the way downtown. Ruth barely listened, though. The only conversation going on in her mind was the one she would soon have to have with Kathy. At least if she went out to karaoke, she'd get to put off the inevitable for a little bit longer. When Val pulled into the parking lot of the Grille, however, she almost didn't find a parking spot. The bar appeared to be filled to its maximum capacity.

Ruth looked around the crowded lot. "Now I *really* don't think this is a good idea," she said.

Val shut off the engine and looked at her. "I know you can sing. I've heard you singing to yourself in the break room."

Ruth felt her cheeks flush. "It's not something I do in front of people. I definitely don't do karaoke. I only sing for myself. It keeps me calm."

"Well, wouldn't it be good to get calm before you have to talk to your sister?"

Ruth had to admit that Val had a point. She opened the passenger door. "Fine. I'll go in, but I'm not promising that I'll get onstage."

Val clapped her hands and then opened the driver's side door. "I know this is exactly what you need. You won't regret it."

Ruth followed as Val led the way into the bar and grabbed a table that had just been vacated in the back. Someone had spilled something on the table, so Val left to retrieve some napkins.

Ruth sat down and watched the karaoke DJ set up the system on the stage at the front of the room. A knot formed in her stomach at the idea of standing up there and belting out some show tune. That wasn't the kind of music she sang when she was alone. The songs she chose were always peaceful. She doubted that the karaoke system had been loaded with any of the songs she knew. After a quick glance around her, she decided that probably no one at the bar would want to hear the kinds of songs she sang anyway.

Ruth eyed the door and thought about escaping before Val came back. After another minute, she decided that, yes, she wanted to go. But she would say goodbye to Val first. She stood and looked around, straining to see over the people in the crowd, but she couldn't find her coworker anywhere.

A moment later, the music started up, and the karaoke DJ invited the first group up onstage. The people who'd been sitting at the table next to Ruth got up and walked over to a game room that was located just off the main bar. Ruth could just make out a dartboard and pool table inside the room.

She looked at her watch. Kathy would be arriving home from work right about now. Her older sister had no idea the news that was coming her way.

Ruth sat back down. She wasn't ready to tell Kathy. She decided that she'd stay for karaoke after all. But only for one song. After that, she'd go home and say what had to be said.

Micah Stolzfus stepped off the intercity bus at the Pittsburgh station. He was halfway home to his Amish community in Lititz, Pennsylvania, and once his five-hour layover was complete, he would be back on his way home again. He frowned at the thought of what was sure to be an uncomfortable return.

Just yesterday his bus had pulled up to Ashland, Ohio, where Micah had traveled for only one purpose. He had gone there to meet the woman who was intended to be his *Fraa*. He was twenty-four years old now, and his parents had grown concerned because he hadn't yet courted anyone. They didn't understand that there were things he wanted to do before he got married. They didn't understand that his dreams did not include living a farmer's life.

They didn't understand that he didn't want to be Amish anymore.

Micah followed the crowd off the bus and was moving toward the station when a flashing light caught his attention. Across the street, a neon sign blinked bright green: Karaoke Tonight.

He'd heard of karaoke before, but he'd never done it. There was no place for karaoke in the simple, plain life of the Amish. Micah knew that there was nothing wrong with singing. But he was pretty sure that the Amish would consider the style of any music offered at such a place to be taboo. The door opened to the bar as someone stepped outside, and the notes of a rock song filtered out into the night air. Micah cocked his head and listened.

Definitely taboo.

"Are you coming inside?"

Micah turned to see the bus driver holding the station door for him. He cleared his throat and swallowed hard. "Actually, I was thinking about going across the street for a bite to eat," he said.

The bus driver dropped his gaze to Micah's black boots and slowly brought it back up over his trousers and blue Amish shirt. He stopped when he reached Micah's straw hat. "Are you sure you want to do that?"

Micah knew he looked different from the people in Pittsburgh. He'd always known, while growing up in Lititz, that he looked different from the *Englisch*. He'd accepted this fact for most of his life. It was only four years ago that this fact had begun to bother him.

"I'm for certain sure," he responded. He'd never had a chance before to see how the other side lived. When he was eighteen and his friends were having their *Rumspringa*, his *Daed* was sick. The responsibility for the farm duties had fallen on his shoulders. Perhaps *Gött* had granted him these five hours now to find out what he'd missed. Micah feared that if he didn't seize the opportunity, he would regret it forever.

The bus driver glanced at his watch, then looked over at the bar. "I could maybe join you for a little while."

Micah realized that the bus driver was worried about him. He shook his head. "If it's all the same to you, this is something I have to do on my own."

The bus driver hesitated, but then shrugged. "Suit yourself. I'm here for another hour if you run into some trouble."

The man's words echoed in Micah's head as he made his way across the street, dodging traffic and standing out like a sore thumb. He could practically feel people's eyes boring into his back as he crossed to the other side and walked through the parking lot. No one expected to see an Amish man going into a bar. But when he opened the door and heard the music, Micah forgot all about what people thought and raced right in.

Micah elbowed his way through the crowd to get to the front where the stage was set. The notes of a country song filled the room as a man onstage sang his heart out. The man was good, but Micah knew he could do better. He hummed along and searched for an empty table. Spying one at the back wall, he headed in that direction. As soon as he took a seat, his knee began to bounce, and his hands tapped the table along with the beat. It was going to be a good night. He didn't even care about all the stares his presence provoked.

When he looked to his left, he saw that the girl at the next table was also watching him. She quickly looked away, but not before he noticed the strange look on her face.

The girl was upset about something. But what?

Micah knew he looked out of place, but his presence surely wasn't threatening anyone. Was it? He'd never spent any time with the Englisch. Perhaps they feared the Amish and he just didn't know it.

"My name is Micah," he said, trying to set her at ease. "Micah Stolzfus."

No response. The young woman continued to look straight ahead at the stage.

"I don't bite. Promise." Micah laughed and took off his straw hat. He held it in one hand and ran his fingers through his hair to clean himself up a bit. "Don't let the clothes fool you. I'm just a typical guy who likes music."

The young woman looked over at the bar, then back toward him. She kept her gaze low, focusing on his hat, which now sat on the table. "Ruth. My name's Ruth."

Micah smiled as he bounced his head with the music. "It's nice to meet you, Ruth. Do you sing?"

She shook her head. "Not in public." She looked at his shirt and suspenders. "I didn't know that the Amish listened to music."

"We don't." He smirked and put his finger to his lips conspiratorially.

She giggled and covered her mouth. He found her response endearing. Her eyes squinted adorably when she laughed.

Micah forced his attention back to the stage. The man who'd been singing country passed the mic over to a young girl who was just stepping up on the stage. The music began again, and the sound she made caused him to cringe.

"Do you come here often?" he asked Ruth.

She giggled again, but he didn't understand why.

"Did I say something funny?"

Her cheeks flushed a pretty pink. "I don't know if you're aware, but that's an old pickup line."

Micah still didn't follow. "What's a pickup line?"

Her eyes widened and filled with surprise. "You know, like if someone wants to ask someone out."

"Huh. I never knew that. We do things a little different where I'm from." He put his hand up in a gesture of assurance. "But just to let you know, I wasn't picking you up. Honest."

They laughed together this time. Ruth was such a sweet person. Now he was even happier that he'd come in tonight.

"And just so *you* know," she said, "I've never been here before. I'd much rather go home after work and read a book. My coworker just dragged me here today because I got fired. She thought I needed a night out."

"I'm sorry to hear that. Losing a job can't be easy."

Ruth shrugged and looked at the stage. "Oh, I'll figure something out." She turned back to him. "So, where are you from?"

"Lititz. My bus leaves in a little over four hours. I just thought I would come in and see how the Englisch entertain themselves. This is my first time in a bar," he admitted.

She smiled. "Mine too." She looked past him into the adjacent game room, and suddenly her smile faded.

Micah followed her gaze and saw that two men were having some sort of argument. "Maybe they're fighting about the game," he said. He cocked his head and listened. It sounded like the argument was about money. One guy owed the other one some kind of debt—a big one, apparently—and the man was calling it due.

Ruth grew pale and stood up, gripping her purse. "I have to go. It was nice to meet you." She turned and nearly bumped right into another woman.

"Oh, no you don't." The woman grabbed Ruth's shoulders. "I've already told the DJ what song you're going to sing. You're next."

"Val, I have to leave."

"Not until you sing. It'll help you take your mind off the bank. You wanted to calm down, remember?" The woman named Val took Ruth's hand and pulled her toward the stage. Micah could hear Ruth trying to convince her friend that she didn't want to sing, and explaining that she really did want to go.

Micah felt like he should do something, but who was he to Ruth? He looked back into the game room. Other men had stepped up and were holding the two arguing men back from each other. Would there be a brawl?

As Micah watched, one of the two men shook himself free and stomped out of the room. He brushed past Micah's table and headed for the bar, where he sat on a stool and ordered a drink. If a scuffle had been brewing, it appeared to have been derailed. Is that what had made Ruth want to leave? Had she not wanted to see a fight? Micah didn't blame her.

He looked up at Ruth, who was standing on the stairs to the stage, waiting for her turn. She was staring at the man at the bar as well. The moment Micah had first noticed her, she'd looked upset. Now, she looked outright fearful.

Micah took another, more careful glance at the drunken man. Why, he wondered, had the man affected Ruth in this way? Why was she afraid of him?

The man was dressed nicely in business pants and a dress shirt. He might have even had a tie on earlier, but his top shirt buttons had since been undone, and his shirtsleeves were rolled up—for darts or fighting, Micah didn't know.

All Micah knew was that sweet Ruth was afraid of this man, and that—between the man's presence and her friend Val's insistence—Ruth was trapped up there as she waited her turn onstage.

CHAPTER TWO

The girl onstage was belting out a song from an old '80s movie, something about taking somebody's breath away. Her singing was off-key, but that wasn't what was making Ruth cringe. As Ruth stood at the base of the stage stairs to wait her turn, she squirmed knowing that Taylor Williams was sitting at the bar. The very same Taylor Williams who'd set her up to be fired. But not before leading her to believe that she truly meant something to him. There had been a short time when he took her breath away too.

Ruth remembered the first time Taylor had pulled his car up to the bus stop after work. It was the only time she'd seen him outside the bank, where he sometimes came to visit his grandfather. When he offered her a ride home, he'd made it sound like he had just been driving by.

How naïve she had been.

Ruth could still hear the sweet and kind words Taylor had uttered during that ride home. Nobody had ever spoken to her in that way. It had never occurred to her that Taylor had even noticed her before. But in the car that day, he'd told her that he really liked the dress she wore the previous Friday. Ruth had felt so special. He had noticed her. Handsome, wealthy Taylor Williams had noticed the boring, nearly broke orphan Ruth Griffin. After a lifetime of being overlooked, Ruth had dared to hope that someone finally saw her. What Taylor actually saw was an easy target. Weeks of buttering her up eventually led up to his request to slip him some money.

It had never occurred to her that being noticed would make her a target for a thief.

Ruth had felt as though Taylor had punched her in the gut. He had asked her to steal. And when she refused, he'd told his grandfather that she was skimming money and got her fired. Mr. Williams had even threatened to press charges. She didn't know what would happen if he made good on that threat. Even without evidence, she had a powerful accuser. And if Taylor somehow convinced the police that she'd made a confession, and if she was somehow convicted . . . Well, then she would be a criminal, just like the person who'd killed her parents.

Ruth couldn't ever break the law, though. She could never be like that murderer. So despite how much Taylor meant to her, she'd ended things with him the very day he'd asked her to steal. The realization that he'd been using her the whole time did nothing to ease her broken heart. For the first time in seven years, since her parents' death, Ruth had felt like she belonged to someone. She had felt valued as a person. In reality, Taylor had seen her as nothing more than an opportunity to steal money.

Now it was her word against his, and Grandpa didn't believe her over Taylor. Deep down, she wondered if the bank president knew what his grandson was like. Did he condone Taylor's lawless ways?

Seeing Taylor bent over the bar now, barely able to stand, she wondered at his state of mind. She wondered, too, why he had needed to steal money in the first place. His family was well-off, so why hadn't he gone to them? Why had he been reduced to using an unsuspecting bank teller who was just trying to build a career? Who simply wanted to live on her own and be self-sufficient? Did Taylor have any idea how his actions had ruined her? Did he even care?

"Get ready!" Val shouted from the sidelines. Ruth suddenly realized that Val didn't know that Taylor was at the bar too. Now, more than ever, Ruth had a valid reason not to get up on that stage and sing. She couldn't let Taylor see her. She eyed the side door and wondered if she could make a run for it.

The song that had been playing ended.

"You're up!" the karaoke DJ shouted to Ruth. "Our next little ditty just might get your toes tapping. Please welcome . . ." He looked at her to introduce herself.

Ruth shook her head.

"She wants to remain anonymous." He laughed. "Uh-oh. That could be good or bad. Brace yourselves, everyone!"

Ruth looked behind her. Val was shooing her with her hands. "Get up there."

Ruth swallowed hard with a gulp and took three steps up onto the platform. The DJ handed her the wireless mic. She tapped it once and heard the speakers throughout the bar make a thump sound.

"It's on." The DJ flipped a switch on the karaoke machine, and the music began. The screen in front of Ruth immediately began scrolling through a set of lyrics that she was supposed to be singing right now but wasn't.

Ruth mouthed the words, but no sound came from her throat. Some people sitting in front looked at her strangely. Those who weren't paying attention kept on doing what they were doing: playing games, talking to each other. Taylor remained hunched over the bar. Ruth was so afraid that he'd turn around and see her that she couldn't take her eyes off him.

"Are you gonna sing, or are you gonna just stand there looking cute?" the DJ asked. His question prompted a few people at the bar to turn around and find out what was going on.

Thankfully, Taylor wasn't one of them.

Ruth shook her head. She whispered, "I can't." Never one for the spotlight, she had always struggled with singing in public and would have done so even if Taylor wasn't at the bar. But this was much worse. She caught a glimpse of Val's encouraging face down in the crowd.

"You love this song!" Val shouted. "Let's hear it, Ruth!"

Ruth shot a glance toward the bar just in time to see Taylor whip around at the mention of her name.

Taylor stepped away from the bar and straightened up. He folded his arms and tilted his head at a threatening angle, as if to say, *Let's hear what you've got.* She wondered what he would do if she refused to sing, just as she'd refused to break the law for him. Would he get her kicked out of here? See that she was banned from the bar permanently? Would she care if he managed to do either of these things?

Ruth glanced at the door again. She could make a run for it. She turned back to the people who were staring up at her. Some, who had already been perturbed by her hesitation, were now openly heckling her. She readied herself to make the dash.

Then she saw Micah stand up at the back.

Ruth locked her gaze on his. She'd never met an Amish person before. The concern on his face looked authentic. But who knew if that was the case? Taylor's sweet words had sounded real too. A long history of trust issues had led Ruth to a life of solitude and isolation. She knew that to be the truth. But that didn't mean she didn't want someone to care about her.

The blue of Micah's shirt brought out the blue of his eyes. He pushed back the blond hair that feathered away from his face. *I never realized that the Amish wear their hair a little longer than normal people,* Ruth thought. She instantly felt guilty for using the word *normal*. Micah appeared to be the only person in this place who felt concern for her. Maybe *he* was the only one who was normal.

She raised a hand in his direction. She wasn't sure why she did it. There was just something about him that made him seem like a lifeline. He took a hesitant step and glanced around the room. Looking at her again, he mouthed the words to the song she was supposed to be singing. Then he took another step, and another, but now he kept his eyes locked on hers as he made his way closer and closer to the stage.

Then she noticed a queasy look come upon his face. He stopped halfway across the room and looked at the exit door. Was he experiencing the same stage fright she was? She wondered if that was something that ever happened to Amish people. She was fairly certain that the Amish didn't ever get on stages. What she was asking him to do went against his way of life. His hesitancy proved this.

"Miss, if you're not going to sing, you have to get off the stage and give someone else a try," the DJ called to her.

Val stood up. "Come on, Ruth, you can do this! You have a beautiful voice. Let everyone hear it."

Ruth looked at Taylor, who was now smirking at her. She could see him laughing, which just made everything he'd done to her feel even worse. She was a joke to him. She had always been a joke to him.

Ruth looked down at the screen and read the next verse to the song. She knew this one by heart. At least Val had chosen a song she knew. Ruth closed her eyes and imagined herself standing in her garden. She let her body sway back and forth and pretended she was skimming her free hand across the top of her pink rose bushes.

She opened her mouth and let a single lyric come out. It was so quiet, it was almost like a whisper through the speakers. She pushed a little more air out and, for the very first time, heard the sound of her own voice being sung into a microphone.

At the sound, she froze.

Her garden immediately vanished from her mind, and her eyes flew open wide. "I'm sorry. I can't do this." She held the microphone out for the DJ to take.

He shook his head. "That was beautiful. We want to hear more. Keep going."

Ruth kept offering the microphone to him. She looked around the crowd, but now instead of disdain and smirks, she saw expressions of awe and eagerness for more.

Not from Taylor, though. One look at him told her that the only emotion he felt toward Ruth was hatred.

The room spun, and Ruth's knees buckled. People's shouts filled her ears, and she knew she was going down.

CHAPTER THREE

Micah knew Ruth needed help. Her voice was beautiful. It had only taken her one line to prove that. But the girl obviously had a horrible bout of stage fright. As an Amish man, he knew the limitations of his *Ordnung* didn't allow him to get on that stage to help her.

But coming to her aid would be an act of charity, he reasoned with himself. Not to mention that he'd already broken the rules by being in the bar in the first place.

When her knees buckled, he understood clearly that she was not well. He knew in that moment that helping her was more important than his need to follow the Amish way.

Micah ran to the stage, taking all three steps in one jump. He caught Ruth under the elbow before she could fall forward. Looking toward the DJ, he lifted a hand and pointed to the extra microphone. The man picked it up and tossed it to him, and Micah caught it with his free hand. He focused on the lyrics on the screen and joined in at the next verse without missing a single beat.

He kept his eyes trained on Ruth, nudging her to join him. Her green eyes held such fear. He lobbied the song's lead back to her with a smile to take away her fright. She closed her eyes briefly and sang the next line with him, but he knew something was holding her back. He wanted her to know there was nothing to be afraid of.

As Micah sang beside Ruth, the lyrics took on a meaning that he'd missed all the times he'd sung the song in private. Before, he'd always thought the song was about love. But now, standing on a stage in front of a crowd of people and holding a petrified Ruth up beside him, he realized it actually was about friendship.

Micah didn't know this woman. Their entire relationship consisted of sharing bits of small talk and laughs over a span of ten minutes, at most. What he did know was that he didn't like seeing the fear on her face. He didn't like seeing how pale her skin became when she looked scared. He didn't like feeling her hand tremble beneath his, or watching her grip the microphone so hard with her other hand that her knuckles went white. She had yet to look at him. Her attention was on something in the crowd. Micah tried to follow her gaze as he continued to sing his heart out.

When he looked into the crowd, he could see people's amazement. They were clearly enjoying his singing. A few of the people wore smiles. He supposed this had something to do with his Amish attire, but those smiles only made him sing louder.

By the third refrain, he realized he had never felt freer. In that moment, Micah knew that he was doing exactly what he had been made to do. It seemed impossible that he could ever go back to working on a farm and hiding this part of himself again.

But he knew that was exactly what he had to do. The Amish way was the only life he had ever experienced, and it was the only life he would ever have.

As that truth hit him, Micah decided that, right then and there, he would fully enjoy this moment of freedom. He most likely would never experience such a moment again. He threw his head back and belted out the last few bars, bringing the song to a tingling crescendo. His eyes closed involuntarily, and he held that final note long after the music had stopped.

There was silence in the whole bar when he finished. As Micah brought his head back down, he felt tears run down his cheeks. He opened his eyes and stared out into the crowd, seeing the many faces before through a blur of moisture.

Then one person broke the silence, clapping slowly. One by one, others joined in until there was a chorus of shouts and applause and demands for him to sing again.

What have I done?

If his family could see him right now, he would be shunned, for certain sure.

At eighteen, Micah had committed to the church and been baptized. He'd made a conscious decision to live the Amish way. He'd also privately decided that he would never let his desire to sing and perform onstage come between him and Gött. The Amish way always pointed to Gött and never to the individual.

Now, standing in the spotlight was pitting him against everything he had agreed to and embraced.

"How about this one?" The DJ put on another song, and the music instantly took hold of Micah. The sound coursed through his veins, causing his body to bounce to the beat.

Suddenly Ruth's hand dropped from his grasp, and she flew down the stairs, still carrying her microphone in her fist. Watching her go, Micah felt torn between going after her and staying behind to sing. What was wrong with him? He wanted to make sure she was okay. But this once-in-a-lifetime opportunity called to him even louder.

Then he saw a man at the bar chase after her. Did they know each other? Perhaps her fright originated from off the stage and not on it.

With the microphone still in her hand, Ruth ran from the building and out into the parking lot. The sounds of her footfalls and hard breathing echoed through the room as they came through the speakers.

Micah sang louder, trying to cover up the sounds, but the audience looked around with confused expressions on their faces. All Micah could do was sing on, and deep down, that was really all he wanted to do. He refocused on the song lyrics and put his whole self into the music.

"Stay away, Taylor! I mean it. Leave me al—!" Ruth's voice cut off as her microphone went out of range.

Micah felt startled. For a moment, he wondered whom Ruth was telling to stay away.

But there was only one answer. The guy from the game room. He was the only one who'd gone after her.

The audience stopped listening to Micah and began to talk among themselves. Micah's voice trailed off. If it weren't for what was happening to Ruth, he'd be happy to stay up on the stage all night. But he had a decision to make: go check on Ruth or keep singing.

Deciding to let the microphone go was harder than he'd thought it would be. How could he have thought he would be satisfied to sing only one song?

But he had no choice. Ruth needed help.

Micah dropped his own mic to the stage floor, took one leap off the stage, and ran for the door.

"Don't come near me, Taylor. I mean it." Ruth tore her arm from his tight grasp. How could she have ever trusted this man? Seeing him now—so intoxicated he could barely stand—made her ill. His typical clean-cut attire had become as disheveled as the rest of his life. His black silky hair fell over one eye, and there in the dark parking lot, lit only by the streetlights, half his face was in shadow.

Taylor Williams was bad news, she had discovered, and in this moment, he fully looked the part. "You have a lot of nerve coming near me after you got me fired."

After you tried to use me.

"All you had to do was push some cash my way. But no, you just had to be a little Miss Goody." As Taylor closed in on her, Ruth could smell alcohol on his breath. She saw that he had a black eye. Apparently, she wasn't the only one he'd upset today.

Ruth realized that Val was still inside, which left her with no way to make a clean escape. She glanced across the street at the bus station and thought about buying a ticket. It would be better than walking. She needed to get someplace where there were people, away from Taylor, and going back into the Grille wasn't an option. Taylor would only follow her there. *If only Val hadn't made me get onstage,* she thought. *Then Taylor wouldn't have ever seen me.*

Taylor laughed. "Serves you right, getting fired. Maybe next time you'll do as you're told." He moved in close again, and when Ruth stepped away, he reached out and grabbed her neck.

Ruth felt her eyes widen in shock. Never before had she been manhandled in such a violent way. "Let me go!"

A new look came into his eyes, and his grip tightened, causing her to gag. Ruth realized that she had to do something before he killed her. She thought of her parents and how they hadn't gotten away from their assailant during a home invasion seven years before. She couldn't wind up like them: murdered in cold blood. Without another thought, she lifted her hands and battered them at his face. She hadn't realized that she still held the microphone, and before she even knew what she was doing, the mic hit Taylor squarely on the side of his head.

Instantly, he let go of her neck and stumbled backward, gripping his head in pain. In the next moment, he tripped and fell backward. He landed hard, and as he did, the back of his head struck the ground.

Ruth stood motionless, frozen by horror at what she had done. She looked at her hand. The microphone was still in her grasp. She stared at it in shock. Her hand seemed as if it belonged to someone else. Never before had she struck anyone, never mind knocked them to the ground. She let go of the mic with a wince, and it hit the pavement with a smack. She rubbed her hands together as if to cleanse them of the stain of assaulting someone.

Taylor groaned and struggled to sit up. He turned onto his side. "You'll pay . . . for . . . that." His words were slurred, but she understood them loud and clear. She needed to get out of there. She didn't know if he was able to hurt her again. But if he could, there was no doubt that he would. As she stood there, trying to decide what to do, Taylor fell forward and landed on his face. He didn't say another word.

A sound from somewhere caused her to whip around. Ruth didn't see anyone coming out of the bar. But the parking lot was filled with cars and dimly lit by a few light posts. Someone could be out there in their car. Someone could have seen what she'd done.

But he had been choking her. She touched her neck where she could still feel his tightening grip. She backed away from Taylor, slowly at first. Then Ruth finally turned and ran toward the street.

Taking off across the parking lot, she ran blindly. When she reached the street, she was nearly hit by oncoming traffic. Horns blared and headlights flashed as she made it to the other side and rushed toward the door of the bus station. On her way, she noticed a bus readying for departure. She ran for its open door and boarded without a glance back. She kept her head down and averted her gaze from anyone in their seats. What if any of them had seen her hit Taylor? She made her way down the narrow aisle and felt grateful to find the last row empty. When she reached it, she fell into it and sank low, trying to shield herself from anyone who could be watching her from outside the windows, as well as from people sitting in the seats ahead of her.

Only then did she realize that her whole body was trembling uncontrollably. She thought she might be sick.

For seven years, she had detested her parents' killer. She'd never understood how anyone could bring themselves to take a life.

But what if she had just done exactly that?

What if she was no better than him?

CHAPTER FOUR

Micah burst out the doors and immediately looked around to see if he could find Ruth. He scanned the parking lot and then looked across the street just in time to catch sight of her popping onto a bus. A glance back at the parking lot showed a man struggling to get up from the ground. It was the guy from the game room.

But why was he on the ground?

It didn't matter. Really, the only thing Micah cared about in that moment was making sure Ruth was safe. He set out for the bus and made it just as the bus doors were about to close.

"Thanks for holding the door," he told the driver. "Can I buy my ticket on here?"

"You too?" The driver glanced to the back where Ruth was just reaching the back seat. He gave an exasperated sigh but nodded and told Micah the price. Once his ticket was paid for, the bus was in gear and backing up before Micah had made it even halfway down the aisle.

Finally, when he reached the end of the bus, he took the seat beside her. He felt her shaking even before he noticed her trembling hands. He took one of them in his own and waited, offering up a silent prayer for Gött to show him how to help her.

Micah had no idea where this particular bus was headed. He also doubted he would be back in time to catch his own. Fortunately, his family wasn't expecting him in the morning. He could catch another bus from some other location—that is, if he got on another bus at all.

When he entwined his fingers with Ruth's, she gripped his hand tighter. Micah felt reassured. He'd made the right choice in coming after her. If there was one thing that was clear to him, it was that Ruth shouldn't be alone right now. Whatever happened back there had scared her. He wondered if she would tell him what had transpired. The fact was, she didn't know him either. Perhaps his presence was enough. Micah decided that it would be up to him to speak first. The key to earning her trust would be to keep it light. But what could he talk to an *Englischer* about? His only frame of reference was living an Amish life on an Amish farm.

So that's where he began.

"I'm the oldest of eight kids," he said quietly. "My parents have already chosen a farm for me. In the Amish community, it's customary for the youngest child to receive the family farm and for the parents to live on the property until their death. But since I'm the oldest, I have to start my own farm." Micah looked at Ruth and saw that she had yet to raise her gaze to him. He wasn't even sure if she was listening. "I hate farming."

Ruth's head lifted slightly at his confession. He took that as a sign she was listening, and this encouraged him to continue.

"To be honest, I'm a big disappointment to my family. I'm twenty-four years old and should be married by now. That's why I'm on the road. My parents arranged for me to marry an Amish girl in Ohio. The problem is, they arranged it with her parents, and then they neglected to tell her. Imagine my surprise when I got there this morning and she told me she wouldn't marry me."

Ruth started to giggle but quickly stopped herself. Her laugh sounded musical to Micah, and he smiled.

"It's all right. You can laugh. It *is* kind of funny. Although, my parents won't be laughing when I get home tomorrow. If I get home tomorrow."

Ruth looked straight at him. Her eyebrows raised in question. Then she frowned. "You didn't have to come with me. You should have stayed. I don't want you to be in trouble."

"That's not what I meant," Micah confessed. "I meant, if I go back at all." He supposed that she probably didn't understand what he was trying to say.

Ruth's head tilted, though, and she squinted her eyes and quickly said, "I see. You're running away."

Micah sighed. "I never thought of it that way. But maybe I'm running *to* something. Does that make sense? All my life I wanted to sing. I wanted to be on the stage and in the spotlight, and tonight was the first time that I dared do it."

"You have a beautiful voice," she whispered. "I don't know if I should say that or not, but you do. It's so powerful."

"So do you," he told her. Even though he really only heard her sing that one line, he knew she was quite talented.

Ruth shook her head. "I shouldn't have been up there. I don't sing in public. My coworker . . ." She shook her head again. "Val shouldn't have pushed me. If only I could speak up for myself. But I've never been able to do that, no matter how hard I try."

Ruth looked out the window, and the headlights of oncoming cars lit her face. Silence grew between them, and Micah wasn't sure what he should say next. He didn't want the conversation to be over.

"Do you know where we're going?" he asked.

She shook her head. "I was so scared."

He waited for her to elaborate. He figured it had to do with that man. "Did he hurt you?"

She touched her neck and nodded. "He . . . Is he dead?"

Micah thought back to the man on the ground. "He was trying to get up when I saw him, so no."

Ruth sighed and leaned back on the seat cushion. "Thank God. I was so scared. He was choking me, and I hit him on the head with the microphone. He fell back and hit the back of his head on the pavement. I had to get out of there." She gave him a sideways glance. "Does that make me a bad person?"

"*Nee*, not at all," Micah told her. "He hurt you. I'm sorry he hurt you. I should have come out sooner. Not that I could have done much, I suppose. The Amish don't fight back."

"The whole 'turn the other cheek' thing?" she asked. "I only have one neck, though. I don't typically fight back either, but it was like my hands had a mind of their own."

"I don't call that fighting back," Micah said. "What you did was more about survival. You can't beat yourself up over it."

She giggled again, and he realized the irony of his phrasing.

"Sorry, poor choice of words. I'm glad to see you're able to laugh now, though."

"Well, now that I know he's fine, I feel a little better. Thank you, Micah. I suppose if you hadn't jumped on the bus, I'd still be here panicking. To be honest, I've never hit anyone before. I still can't believe I did it."

"I understand. I can't imagine hitting anyone either."

She studied his face for a few minutes in the dim light. Part of her face was cast into a shadow, but he could see her squinting at him.

"Is there something wrong?" he asked. "Do I have something on my face?"

She shook her head and smiled slightly. "I just can't believe I'm sitting on a bus with an Amish person having this conversation. This is literally the second-worst day of my life, but having an Amish person come to my aid makes it even more surreal. I feel like this is a nightmare, but you're maybe the least scary person I've ever met. If I woke up from this nightmare . . . Well, that would mean that you would go away too, and somehow, I think that would be unfortunate. That doesn't make sense, does it? We don't even know each other."

"We do now, and I'm not a dream," Micah told her gently. "But you said this was the second-worst day of your life, so now I have to ask, What could be worse than this?"

Ruth looked back toward the window.

Immediately, Micah felt a rush of remorse. "I'm so sorry. You don't have to answer that. It's none of my business." Micah could have kicked himself for being so personal. He wished he could take his words back.

Ruth didn't look at him, but spoke while facing the window. "When I was fourteen, my parents were killed in a home invasion. I had to go live with my sister, who's ten years older than me. She wasn't thrilled with the arrangement then, and she still isn't. I had almost gotten to a place where I could finally get my own apartment. Everything fell apart today. The man back there . . . the one I hit? He set me up to get fired."

"So you *did* know him," Micah said. At her nod, he continued, "You were afraid of him even before he attacked you in the parking lot. That's the reason you wouldn't sing, isn't it?"

"Yes," Ruth said. "I didn't want him to see me. I should have left as soon as I saw him in the game room. But Val wouldn't take no for an answer."

Micah shook his head. This was all so much to process. "I have never had to deal with anything like this in Lititz. I'm sorry about your parents. That must have been worse than a nightmare." Micah couldn't imagine any such horror coming anywhere near his family farm. "Did the police catch the person?"

"No. They believe it was gang related. Maybe some kind of initiation ritual. Not knowing makes it even worse and harder to get over."

"I imagine harder to forgive as well," he said quietly.

Ruth turned her questioning gaze onto him. "I don't understand. What do you mean?"

Micah wasn't sure if he had said something wrong. He remembered that he really didn't know Ruth. He was also reminded that he didn't understand the Englisch ways. What he did know, though, was that forgiveness is something Gött requires.

"Perhaps I'm saying this wrong," he started. "The Amish way is to forgive—not because we condone violence and poor behavior, but because forgiving others brings us peace."

Ruth scrunched her nose and shook her head. "I can't imagine how forgiving my parents' killer would help me."

Micah shrugged. "Has *not* forgiving him helped you?"

Ruth turned back to the window and said no more. He could almost feel a wall rise up between them. The silence felt even louder to him than the bus's engine. Micah had an overwhelming urge to race back to his family farm. He obviously didn't understand how things worked outside his Amish community. If he was going to leave the Amish lifestyle, this was something that he had better learn quickly.

But what if, in offending Ruth, he had just burned the only bridge he had to the Englisch world?

Peace? Ruth hardly knew what peace looked like, let alone how to achieve it. And if finding peace meant that she would have to forgive her parents' killer, she doubted she would ever manage it.

Ruth also wondered if Micah meant that she needed to forgive Taylor for getting her fired. Did he also think she should forgive

Taylor for choking her? A shiver ran up her spine, and she trembled just thinking about the attack again. Her chest felt tight, and she forced herself to take a deep breath. As the minutes ticked by, neither she nor Micah said a word. She wasn't trying to be rude; she just didn't understand what he was saying, exactly. And she really didn't think he understood what he was asking of her.

After some time had passed, Ruth felt calm enough to speak again. "Taylor Williams is the bank president's grandson. He would come through my line when I was a teller and tell me things." She stopped, unable to continue.

"What sorts of things?" Micah asked.

Ruth shrugged. "Just a bunch of lies. He would flatter me, saying things like I was pretty."

Micah tilted his head, and she realized he didn't have his straw hat anymore. He must've left it back on the table. She suddenly felt guilty as she realized that he also didn't have his bag. He had left everything behind to help her, a complete stranger.

"Anyway," she went on, "a couple weeks ago, I was promoted. I couldn't believe it. I thought things were really turning around for me. I was finally going to make enough to get my own place to live. I think it was the first time Kathy smiled since I came to live with her seven years ago." Ruth rubbed her forehead. "I was so dumb. So naïve. I actually thought Taylor would propose and that we would get married. He said he loved me." Ruth faced Micah straight on. "And then he asked me to break the law. He wanted me to slip him money, but I couldn't do it." She shook her head. "I just couldn't do it."

"So, you got fired because you *wouldn't* break the law?" he asked.

She made a small scoffing sound. "That's not what I was told. He told his grandfather, Mr. Williams, I had been stealing from the bank. I didn't steal anything, but my word didn't mean anything. Today before closing, Mr. Williams pulled me into his office and said to pack up my things and go home. I can see now that I never meant anything to Taylor. He was pretending to care the whole time."

"Whoa," Micah said, leaning back on the seat cushion. "There's so much wickedness in the world. Part of me says that I should go back to my community and forget my reluctance, but another part of me knows there is more goodness out here than evil. Though, I suppose it isn't always easy to find it. It seems to me that music helps. I know it has the power to bring people together. Music can heal."

Ruth thought about this. It was true: certain songs she sang did help with her anxiety. But heal? She wasn't sure about that.

She laughed at the thought. "I can't imagine any song healing someone as corrupt as Taylor."

Micah was quiet for a moment. Finally, he said, "Did you tell Taylor's grandfather about all the things he did?"

She shook her head. "Sort of. I told him I didn't steal anything, but when he didn't believe me, I didn't push it. I didn't get into everything Taylor had done. It didn't seem worth it. I've always struggled with speaking up for myself. It's like the words are in my head, but I can't make them come out of my mouth."

"Kind of like when you were onstage tonight."

She nodded. "It's just that the words never sound the same way that I imagine them in my head. Whether I'm speaking them or singing them, they always seem to come out wrong."

Micah twisted to face her and grabbed her hand. "I disagree. You have a lovely voice." Suddenly, Micah sang the song again, this time quietly, just for her ears. His voice was so melodic, she found it mesmerizing. She could almost believe he was singing the words of love to her. Then he nodded and encouraged her to join him.

Ruth shook her head quickly, but he put his finger under her chin and smiled as he sang on. She cleared her throat and took a deep breath, then let it out slowly. Then she opened her mouth and joined him for the refrain. She cringed at the sound of her own voice, but Micah's enthusiasm kept her going.

By the time they'd finished the song, they were both smiling. "All right, maybe you're right about the whole healing thing," she admitted. "I do feel better."

Suddenly she felt a vibration in the back pocket of her pants as her cell phone rang.

Micah looked confused as he glanced around. "It's not me," he said. "I don't have a phone."

"It's mine. I forgot I had it in my pocket." Ruth reached behind her and pulled out her phone. "It's my sister. She's probably wondering where I am." A nauseous feeling swept over Ruth. She braced herself for her sister's rebuke as she clicked a button to answer the call. "Hey, Kathy. I'm running late tonight."

"Where are you?" Kathy yelled through the phone. Ruth pulled it away from her ear and looked at Micah in shock.

"I'm on a bus." Ruth decided not to mention that she had no idea where that bus was going.

"The police were just here, looking for *you!*"

The police? Had they come to interview her about the money that was missing at the bank? The repercussions of Taylor's lies were reaching further than Ruth had expected. "But I didn't do anything wrong."

"A man is dead, and witnesses are saying you hit him!"

Ruth felt a chill fall over her. She'd only ever struck one person. "Taylor's dead? How is that possible?" Ruth looked at Micah, who shook his head.

"He was alive last I saw him," Micah whispered.

"Who is that? Who are you with?" Kathy demanded to know. "It's just a friend."

"You don't have any friends." Kathy's dig cut deep. Why did her sister always have to be so mean? *Well, maybe if you were nicer, more people would stick around to be my friend.* Ruth thought those words, but she knew she would never say them. She never said any of the things she thought.

"You know what? Never mind. Just get back here. I'm not cleaning up your mess."

Ruth began to tremble again. Micah covered her hands with both of his.

"What's going on?" he asked as she hung up the call.

"Taylor's dead, and I killed him." Tears pricked Ruth's eyes. "I think this might be my worst day after all."

CHAPTER FIVE

Throughout his life, Micah had repeatedly heard that the world outside his Amish community was the devil's playground. But he'd never understood what that term meant until this moment. He'd always pushed back on that judgment. It seemed like it was just something the church elders said to keep people from leaving the community. But after seeing everything Ruth had gone through tonight, it occurred to him that maybe the church elders were correct.

If they were, though, how could he ever leave the Amish lifestyle for such a wicked place? He decided that he simply had to believe that there was good in the Englisch world, and he knew deep down that he could find it.

The bus pulled up to the Punxsutawney station. Ruth had already called the police, and they'd told her they would meet her there. Since that call, she hadn't said another word to Micah. But she did let him hold her hand during the last half hour of the trip.

"It's time to go," Micah told her quietly. He looked out the window. Two police cruisers were parked outside the station. "They're waiting for you."

"Do you think they'll arrest me?" Her voice squeaked.

"I don't see how. It was self-defense, and he wasn't dead when you left him. You did what you had to do to get away. I'm going to tell them that. I saw him with my own eyes. Come on, I'll be right next to you." Micah stood and pulled her up, then led her down the aisle and off the bus. They joined three police officers who were standing by the doors to the station.

"Miss Griffin?" One of the officers stepped forward. He wasn't wearing a uniform like the other two. "I'm Detective Styles. Thank you for calling us and meeting with us. We just have a few questions about what happened tonight."

Micah said, "Sir, I can attest to the fact that the man was alive. I saw him getting up off the ground."

All three officers looked his way. Their confused glances traveled up and down his body. He knew it made no sense for an Amish man to be vouching for Ruth. The detective took out a notepad and pen.

"Can I have your name?" he asked.

"Micah Stolzfus. I'm from Lititz. I had a layover before my next bus."

The officer standing behind the investigator said, "And you decided to go to the bar? Forgive me, but is that allowed?"

Micah didn't want to get into the details of his Ordnung. "I went to see the singing for karaoke night. What's important, though, is that I saw Taylor Williams get back up after the incident. Ruth was already on the bus by that time. But also, the man hurt her."

The investigator asked Ruth, "Just how did he hurt you?"

Ruth sighed and touched her neck. "He attacked me in the parking lot and grabbed my neck. He choked me. I raised my hands to push him back and didn't realize I had the microphone still in my hand. I hit him with the microphone and then dropped it."

"And you got away?" the man asked.

"I ran as fast as I could and got on the first bus that was leaving. I just wanted to get away from him. He hurt me. But I didn't kill him. Honest. I just stunned him, and he fell backward."

The investigator looked at Ruth over his pad of paper. "Do you have a history with Taylor Williams?"

"History?" Ruth looked uncomfortable. "He came through my line at the bank a few times."

Micah thought she should tell the whole truth about how Taylor Williams wanted her to break the law. But although he wondered why she wasn't explaining the situation, he let her direct the conversation.

The investigator asked, "Has he bothered you before this evening?"

Ruth dropped her gaze to her hands, which were clasped in front of her. She nodded. "I guess I could say he was stalking me. He pretended to be interested in me."

"I see. Did you return the interest?"

Ruth frowned. "I suppose I believed him." She lifted her head and looked at the investigator. "I'm really shy, and it's not too often someone is interested in me. I guess I'm also naïve."

The investigator slapped his pad shut and nodded. He pocketed his pad and pen in the breast pocket of his suit coat. Then he removed a business card from the pocket and passed it over to her. "Thank you for contacting us and explaining the situation." He looked over at Micah. "Thank you for sharing what you know as well. If either of you can remember anything else, give me a call. And I have your number, Ruth. I'll be in touch if I need to speak with you again."

As the officers turned to leave, Ruth asked, "Can you tell me how Taylor died?"

The investigator shook his head. "An autopsy will have to be done before I can release that information. I'd advise you not to leave the state, though. Until we know the answer to that question."

The men climbed into their cars and left the station parking lot. Ruth let out a deep sigh of relief.

"I thought for sure they were going to arrest me." She looked at Micah. "What do you suppose they meant about not leaving the state? Do you think they still see me as a suspect?"

Micah shrugged. "Honestly, I don't know. Everything about this evening is beyond anything I've experienced."

"Thank you for speaking up for me. That really meant a lot, and I was so glad not to have to do this alone." She took another deep breath and let it out slowly. "And now I have to call my sister back. I have to tell her what happened and ask her to come get me."

Ruth walked away from the doors to make her call. Micah stayed back to allow her some privacy for her conversation. As he waited, he thought about what his next move should be. He didn't want to go back to Lititz. He looked around him and wondered if maybe Punxsutawney was the place where he should start over. It was the place where, every year, the Englisch looked to a groundhog to determine how much longer winter would last. Micah never understood how the practice was supposed to prove anything. It was one of those rituals that confused the Amish. A season was a season, and a shadow didn't shorten it, no matter how much attention Punxsutawney drew. As famous as the town was, though, it wasn't famous for music. He doubted it was the place he was looking for.

Growing up, he'd always pictured himself landing in a place like New York City or Nashville. He never thought he would actually go, though, and even now wondered if he could really do it. He walked inside the bus station.

"How much is a ticket to Nashville?" he asked the clerk behind the glass.

She gave him a price, but just as he took out his wallet to pay, Ruth stepped up behind him.

"I've been kicked out of my home," she said quietly with tears in her eyes. "Micah, I have no place to go. What am I going to do?"

Micah followed Ruth over to a row of chairs in the waiting area. She seemed very upset. But what ideas could he offer her, really? He had no idea what Englischers did when they were put out on the street.

She sat in her chair and began to chew on her thumbnail. "I have no other family," she explained. "Kathy was all I had, and she won't let me come back."

"Did she say why?" Micah asked. "You really haven't done anything wrong. Where I'm from, it's possible to be shunned, but only if we go against our Ordnung."

Ruth stopped chewing on her nail. "'Ord' what?"

"Ordnung. It's a set of rules established by our elders that our community must follow. For example, once we've been baptized, we can't ever leave the community. If we do, then we can't go back again."

"Have you? Been baptized, I mean?"

Micah nodded and frowned. "You see my dilemma? It appears we're in the same place. Both of us stand at a door, and neither of us knows what's on the other side."

She slumped in her chair. "I have no choice but to find out what's on the other side. I've been thrown out of my door. Two doors, actually. First, the bank's, and now the door of my home."

"That doesn't sound very family-like."

Ruth made a sputtering sound. "Family's complicated in my case, I'm afraid. My sister and I have different fathers. Our mom and Kathy's dad divorced when she was young. Kathy and my dad didn't get along, even after our mom married him. So when she was eighteen, she went to live with her dad. I was eight years old at the time. Once my parents were killed, Kathy became my only living relative. Both my sets of grandparents had passed by that time. Kathy wasn't happy to have a fourteen-year-old girl bunking with her. We barely knew each other. I've really overstayed my welcome by still being there at age twenty-one. Taylor's death seems to have been the last straw."

"How so?"

"She said she can't handle the fact that I'm involved with someone's death. She told me she didn't sign up for that kind of publicity, and she can't take the backlash she'll get for keeping me under her roof."

"Did you tell her you can't support yourself? That you lost your work?"

Ruth's eyes teared up. "She said I probably deserved it."

Micah reached for her hand and gave it a squeeze. "Nee, that's not the truth."

Ruth wiped a tear away. "It doesn't matter if it is or isn't. Either way, I'm still unemployed and now homeless. How could she turn me away?"

"My parents would do the same thing if I made the choice not to return," Micah admitted. "If I ever tried to contact them again, they would shun me."

"Shun?" Ruth gave him a look of concern. "What does that mean, exactly?"

"It means to cut someone off, separate them out. It's not a pleasant experience," he said grimly. "Essentially, it means they wouldn't treat me like family anymore." Micah let go of her hand and rubbed the fabric of his black trousers. "I'm not sure I could handle being treated like that. I've seen it done a few times, and it always upsets me. But I also understand order has to be kept in a community that depends on people being there for each other. So, I know that if I were to make that decision, I could never go back. It would just be too painful to try."

Ruth nodded. "If it feels anything like what I'm feeling right now from my sister, I understand." She tilted her head. "But why wouldn't you want to go back? Is it really that bad to live in a community with rules?"

Micah shook his head. "Honestly, I don't know any other way. Maintaining order keeps everyone content, except in those moments when we have to hide certain things about ourselves because they wouldn't be accepted. Then, order feels like a prison."

Ruth's eyes widened at his confession. "I don't even want to think about prison," she said. "What if the police decide they think *I'm* the one who killed Taylor?" She gave a little shudder. "What if I *did* kill him?"

"Then it would be self-defense," Micah said firmly. "I don't think you have anything to worry about."

She sighed. "I hope you're right. I just keep hearing that detective telling me to not leave the state. What do you suppose he meant by that?"

Micah was at a loss. He knew nothing about the Englisch justice system. "I don't know. I wish I could make it all go away for you, but if I was giving out wishes, I'd also have to wish for a bride to make my parents happy." He smiled and winked.

Ruth giggled, and he appreciated the sound. "Did anyone ever tell you that your laughter sounds like music?"

She shook her head and pressed her lips tight. "You're only saying that because you're a musician."

He frowned. "I *want* to be a musician, but I'm supposed to be a husband and farmer. I'll admit, I'm dreading going back to my family without the person they arranged for me to marry. My Daed is going to be very upset."

"Will he shun you?"

Micah shook his head. "Nee, shunning is for graver offenses. They'll just be disappointed."

Ruth leaned back in her seat and looked to the ceiling. "Aren't we a sore bunch? You have a home to go to but don't want to. I want a home, but I don't have one."

Micah sat quietly for a moment, then the clerk at the ticket window called out to him, "Sir, were you going to buy the ticket to Nashville? The bus leaves in ten minutes." He looked at Ruth, who had yet to take her eyes off the ceiling. Getting on that bus would mean leaving her behind with no place to go. It would also mean that he'd made the decision to never go home again. The idea turned his stomach.

Maybe he couldn't do it. Or maybe, he just wasn't ready yet.

"I need a little more time," he whispered.

Ruth angled her head toward him. "Why don't you just tell your parents you want to be a musician? Maybe they'll understand."

Micah shook his head. "The only person who knows is my little sister. And she's sworn to secrecy." An image of little nine-year-old Daisy flashed in his mind. "What am I thinking?" he muttered. "I'm the oldest of eight kids. They look to me as a role model. How can I abandon them?"

This time, Ruth was the one who took his hand. "Trust me when I tell you that family is important. More important than you may realize now. I won't tell you what to do, but I will tell you this: life without them will be harder than anything you can imagine."

Micah took a deep breath and let Ruth's words sink in. "I won't say that I won't ever leave," he said after a moment. "But if I do leave, I'll need to prepare my siblings first. I'm not giving up my dream," he told himself aloud. "I'm just putting it on hold." He stood and turned to the teller. "When is the next bus to Lititz?"

The teller looked at her screen and moved her computer mouse. "That bus leaves in forty minutes. You want a ticket?"

"Two," Micah responded in an instant, then looked at Ruth. The expression on her face mirrored the shock he felt. "I can't leave you here," he said reasonably. "And you won't be leaving the state, so you won't be in trouble with the police."

She sat up straight. "But what happens to me when we get there?"

Micah shrugged. How could he answer that, when he didn't even know what would happen to him when he returned without his bride?

CHAPTER SIX

Ruth slept restlessly beside Micah as the bus drove throughout the night. The sight of the Welcome to Lititz sign when they hit the city limits only caused a feeling of dread to rise up in him. He could feel his plans to become a musician evaporate. Although he tried to tell himself that he would prepare his siblings and leave at a later date, deep down he knew it would never happen. He might as well accept that he would live the life of a farmer and give up his dreams of singing, forever. It wouldn't be long before his parents found him a new Fraa. And he knew they wouldn't care if he was attracted to the woman or not.

He gazed at Ruth's soft complexion. Her long brown hair was mussed. In the Amish community, the women always wore their hair in a tight bun beneath their *Kapps*. Only a husband would ever see his wife's hair loose like this. How simple it would be if Ruth were Amish. Then he could marry her. He could give her a home. He could give her a family.

And then what would he do when the dream to leave Lititz rose up in him again? Was it possible that he'd actually be able to bring himself to go, someday?

If that happened, would he leave Ruth, then, too?

Ruth stirred and turned his way. Her eyes opened and closed a few times. She said in a groggy voice, "Are we there yet?"

"*Ja,* we're pulling up to the bus station now."

She sat up and took out her phone. "Six a.m.," she said. "Not one text from my sister."

The cell phone captured Micah's attention, reminding him that Ruth was, in fact, very Englisch. She would never fit in with the Amish, so thinking about marrying her had been foolish. Just bringing her with him at all had probably been unwise. But arriving home alone somehow seemed worse.

"Would it be too difficult for you to give up the comforts of your world?" he asked.

"I don't really have a choice, do I? I don't have a home."

"I don't mean those kinds of comforts." He nodded at the phone in her hand. "I mean things like the cell phone."

She stared at the device. "Honestly, I probably wouldn't miss it too much. I really only used it for work. Why do you ask?" She lifted her gaze to him.

"Well, you won't be able to use it in my community. You'll have to give up Englisch ways while you're there. Beyond that, I'm not really sure how this will work. I've been thinking about it all night, and I haven't come up with any kind of plan that makes sense," he admitted. "I can't leave you alone. But I also can't bring an Englischer home. My family will be expecting Rachel Miller. It's going to be difficult once I show up without her. I'd suggest that you just pretend for a while to be Rachel, but eventually they would find out."

Ruth made a scoffing sound. "Not eventually. *Immediately.* I don't know how to be Amish."

She had a point, Micah realized. His family would take one look at her and know she was an imposter. Even before she opened her mouth, they would know. They'd have to be blind not to see it. The moment that thought hit him, Micah got an idea.

"Wait. My aunt Connie is blind and a spinster."

"And you want me to hide in her house?" Ruth looked at him incredulously. "I'm sure she would hear me."

Micah laughed. "No, silly, you can pretend to be Rachel and live with her. We're not married, so living together would be a sin. Rachel would have to stay someplace else anyway. Making that place Aunt Connie's house just makes it easier for you to go undetected."

"I'm pretty sure lying is also a sin," Ruth said. "And why aren't we married, anyway? Aren't they going to be expecting you and Rachel to be married?"

"They aren't expecting me at all," Micah said, answering her second question first. "When I arrived in Ohio yesterday, Rachel turned me away immediately. She wasn't having any of it. If I had stayed, our wedding wouldn't have been for another week. We would've come home to Lititz after that.

"As for lying?" he continued. "Well, leaving you alone with no place to go feels like a bigger sin to me. There has to be a way to make this work. I know you could learn Amish ways from Connie. She's blind, but she'll still need some explanation. We can simply tell her that your family runs a business, not a farm. And that you didn't grow up Amish, but your family converted. That should satisfy her.

"As for why we've come back unmarried in the first place, I can just say that Rachel—that *you*—want to get to know me first before marriage. That will be acceptable. What *won't* be acceptable," Micah said, "is that we traveled unchaperoned. Still, I'll take that scolding over returning empty-handed any day."

Ruth's eyes widened. "I won't know any of these rules from your ording."

"Ordnung," he corrected her.

"See? I can't even get that right."

"Don't worry. Living with Aunt Connie will give you time to learn the ways and the language and the rules. It will only be for a few weeks, maybe a month or two. During that time, you'll look for another place to live in Lititz, and I'll prepare my siblings for my departure. I'll come by each day and teach you the ways of the Amish. I'll make it look like we're courting, and no one will find it suspicious or inappropriate. In fact, they'll expect it, since we're betrothed."

Her eyebrows rose. "We're not actually getting married, though, right?"

He smiled at her worried expression. "Nee, we'll call it off once you find a place. Then I can even use our breakup as a reason to leave permanently." The pieces of the plan seemed to fit together perfectly. Micah wanted to set it in motion. It occurred to him that this could really work. He stood and offered his hand to help her up.

She just stared at his hand. Noticing her pale complexion, he finally realized that she wasn't on board.

Micah sat back down, but he wasn't ready to give up yet. "Ruth, you have to see it's the safest thing for you. Where else will you go? A shelter? If that's what you want, I'll bring you to one. But I'm offering you the safest place you can imagine. No one would ever think to look for you in an Amish community."

Her questioning look hit him hard in the gut.

"Why do you think I need a safe place?"

Micah took her hand gently. "You feel you were set up to be fired. What makes you think you won't be set up to take the blame for murder?"

Her mouth hung wide at his words. "But Taylor's the one who set me up at the bank, and now he's dead. Who would set me up to get blamed for his death?"

Micah shrugged. "I don't know, honestly. What I do know is you're alone and need help." He extended his hand again. "Let me help you."

Ruth hesitated for a few more seconds before taking his hand. She gave him a quick nod. "All right," she said. "And I will help you."

Micah smiled at his new friend. The moment he had stepped off his bus last night, his life had changed. He hadn't exactly belonged in that bar, but Gött used him in that place anyway. Gött knew the desires of Micah's heart. He had created Micah to love music, and last night He used that gift to pull him into a place where he was needed. Where *Ruth* had needed him.

He felt a wave of hope wash over him. "I have a feeling we're both going to get the life we always wanted," he said confidently. "This plan will work, I just know it."

Ruth didn't look so sure. "That's easy for you to say. You're not the one having to pretend you're someone you're not. Micah, you've been speaking English to me, but I've heard other non-English words from you too. I don't even know what language the Amish speak."

Micah smiled. "Pennsylvania Dutch. It will be one of the things I teach you. For now, we'll just say that you recently moved to your Ohio community from the Northwest, and that you weren't born Amish. We'll tell them that you were born in Colorado and then moved to the Northwest. . . . That should offer a sufficient explanation for your accent. Amish children don't learn English until school. So it will make sense that your Dutch isn't perfect, and that you prefer English. Just pretend to be shy, and no one will expect you to speak."

"Being shy will be the only thing I'm *not* pretending about." Ruth still looked unconvinced, but she stood and let him lead her out down the aisle of the bus.

"You're going to be fine . . . *Rachel*," Micah said. He turned and winked at her. "Might as well get used to the name. It's nice to meet you, Rachel. We're going to do great things together."

Great things? Ruth sat in the taxi's back seat with Micah beside her and wondered how anything great could come out of this farce. The driver pointed the car out of downtown Lititz, and soon they were passing by the city's homes and colleges. Before long, the landscape changed to rolling hills of grass and wide-open spaces. Every mile took them deeper into rural Lititz, and with every mile her anxiety heightened.

Micah had asked her if she would be willing to give up her phone. But a cell phone was just one of many things she'd need to give up in order to make this work.

"How do I say hello?"

"*Guder Daag*," he replied. "That's an easy one. Just like 'good day.'" His smile expressed his excitement, but this still seemed to her like a terrible idea.

"How do you say 'It's nice to meet you'?" Ruth was pretty sure this charade would be over shortly after they got to his aunt's house.

"*Ich bin froh dich zu aadreffe.*"

Ruth knew her mouth was hanging wide. "You have got to be kidding me. Micah, I can't do this." Her voice grew high and thin.

He took a close look at her face and grabbed her hand. "This is going to work. Trust me. You're going to love Aunt Connie. She's my mother's sister, but everyone knows she's the fun sister. And I know she's going to love you."

"Why didn't she ever get married?"

Micah shrugged. "In the Amish community, there's a small window of time for courting. Because of her blindness, she wasn't well suited to be a farmer's wife. That's the story, anyway. But later I found out there was more to it than that. She loved someone, but because of his parents, it didn't work out."

Ruth inhaled at the idea. "That's horrible. And she never married, so she didn't get to have a family of her own. She must do fine on her own, yes?"

"Ja," Micah said.

"Ja," Ruth practiced the word on her tongue, forcing herself to memorize the feel of the sound. She'd heard him say no as *nee*. Those were important words to know. If nothing else, she could always respond to questions with yes and no. Maybe nobody would notice that she never elaborated.

Yeah, right.

"Your family is going to think I'm a simpleton."

"Why do you say that?" Micah asked. "You seem smart to me."

"That's because I can speak freely with you. But if I do that with the others, I'll give myself away. Micah"—she turned to face him—"you must see this isn't going to work."

"We already talked about how we'll handle the accent." He frowned at her hesitance. "I'm not worried. And I really think you will be a blessing to Connie. I know she always wanted a *Dochder*. Daughter."

"You're in denial. And you're fantasizing." She couldn't help keeping her frustration out of her voice. She took a deep breath and let it out slowly. "I'm sorry. I just feel awful lying to people. How do you say 'sorry'? I have a feeling I'm going to need that one a lot as well."

"*Es dutt mer Leed.*" Micah frowned, and some of his excitement extinguished from his eyes. "Maybe this won't work," he admitted. "But then again, maybe it will. I'll get you into the house with a quick introduction and usher you to a bedroom so that you can change clothes. I'll tell Connie you lost your bag on the trip and want to get out of your travel clothes. I'm sure she'll loan you some of her things. While we're doing all that, I'll see how she reacts to meeting you. Then I'll know whether we can proceed or not. Does that make you feel better?"

Ruth thought about the plan. It was reasonable. "Yes. I mean, ja." At least he wouldn't be taking her straight to his parents. If things didn't go well, that would probably be the end of it, and to a shelter she would go.

His smile came back. "Perfect." He looked out her window and nodded. "Do you see that white house and red barn way out there?"

She followed his gaze. The scene before her was so peaceful. "What a beautiful place. It's so quaint. I've never seen anything like it in Pittsburgh. It's like a painting."

"That's my family's farm."

She whipped her head to look at him in astonishment. "I can't believe you ever wanted to leave. That huge house is *yours*? All this land belongs to your *family*?"

His smile fell from his face again. He shrugged and looked away from her. "It doesn't matter how great a house is, and how many people live in it. It can still be lonely when you're not understood."

Ruth instantly felt regret over her callous words. She certainly knew how it felt to be silenced. "I'm sorry. I mean, *Es . . . dutt . . . mmmm . . .*"

"*Es dutt mer Leed,*" he said with his smile returning.

"*Es dutt mer Leed.*" She reached for his hand. "Friends?"

He said, "*Ferien.* And ja. I couldn't do this without you."

"I just hope we can do it at all."

The car drove on over the rolling hills. The cab driver called back, "The next right?"

"Ja, *danki,*" Micah said.

"What does that mean?" Ruth whispered. "And how does he understand you?"

"He's a taxi driver in Lititz. He encounters a lot of Amish who can't drive cars and need to get around just like everyone else. *Danki* means 'thank you.'"

Ruth practiced the word quietly under her breath. It was also a word she planned to use quite frequently. She went through her growing vocabulary and practiced each word she'd learned so far.

"I feel good about these words. I think I remember them."

"*Gut*," Micah said, teaching her a new one. "You're a fast learner, Rachel."

Ruth rolled her eyes. "I hope I remember to answer to that name."

The driver pulled into a short driveway that led to a small, one-story house that Ruth understood belonged to Connie. There was a wooden fruit stand by the road that said "Produce, Pies, and Crafts."

"That'll be twenty-four dollars," the driver told them over his shoulder.

Micah took out his wallet and paid the driver as Ruth stepped from the car and stared at what would be her home for the next few weeks. A white fence surrounded a small garden off to the side of the house, which was painted an inviting, cheery yellow. The surrounding foliage on the many trees had turned to autumn reds and golds, which gave the property a warm glow.

By the time the taxi pulled out of the driveway and disappeared over the next hill, Ruth had yet to take one step closer to the house. Micah walked over and stood beside her. She felt thankful that he was giving her time before going in.

"Ruth, I appreciate you doing this for me."

She angled a smile his way, feeling glad to hear him call her by her real name in this moment. "But I know you're helping me just as much. Shall we go in?"

"If you're ready." At her nod, he took her hand and led her up the driveway and path to the front door.

With each step, Ruth felt a rising desire for this to somehow work. She wondered why she suddenly felt this way. What had changed since the moment she stepped out of the taxi?

Micah knocked on the door and then opened it. "Aunt Connie," he called, "it's just me. I have someone I want to introduce you to. I brought Rachel to stay with you. I hope that's *gut* with you."

Ruth heard the sounds of the woman stand from a creaking chair in another room. This was followed by the sound of feet shuffling along wood floors, and then Connie appeared in the doorway. Ruth had expected her to be elderly, but Connie couldn't have been more than fifty years old.

She wore a purple dress and a small white bonnet on her head. She resembled Micah and had a beautiful smile. It seemed like she was looking right at Ruth.

Ruth glanced down at the work clothes she still wore. Her black pants and white blouse were the furthest thing possible from Amish attire. Would Connie be able to tell what she was wearing?

Micah said something else in his own language that Ruth didn't understand. The two of them went back and forth for a few moments. Ruth could only assume Micah was relaying all they had planned to say to make this work.

"*Wunderbaar! Ich bin froh dich zu aadreffe,*" Aunt Connie said as she approached the two of them with arms wide open. "*Komm,* child, you are *willkumm* here! I'll try to remember your Pennsylvania Dutch is not strong."

Connie put one arm around Ruth and one arm around Micah and pulled them in for a hug. As Ruth submitted to the embrace, she suddenly realized why she wanted to succeed in this endeavor. In that first moment when she was squished up between Micah and Connie, Ruth found that the hug made her feel like she was family. Family was something that Ruth hadn't experienced since she was fourteen years old.

And family was all that Ruth had ever wanted.

CHAPTER SEVEN

Ruth was left to change in a small bedroom at the back of the house. From there, she could hear Micah talking to his aunt in the front room about his first encounter with Rachel.

He meant with *her*.

Everything he said was a complete fabrication, though, and there was no mention of karaoke night at the Grille. She paid close attention to his words, knowing she would need to tell the same story.

Ruth stood close to the closed door and with her palms pressed against the cool wood. Once they started talking about people in the community, however, Ruth allowed herself to step back and take stock of her temporary new room.

It was a simple bedroom with a narrow, single bed and a nightstand with no lamp on it. There was also no light on the ceiling. There was only one window to allow daylight in, and Ruth knew that come nightfall, the room would be very dark. Her limited knowledge of Amish people told her that they had no electricity and depended on lanterns. But a blind person like Aunt Connie would surely have no need for lanterns. Ruth wondered about all the things she would need while she stayed there, light only being one of them. She hadn't been to the kitchen yet to see if there was even running water.

She lowered her gaze to two dresses that Micah had laid on the bed. Connie bought their reason for Ruth's lack of baggage without batting an eye. One dress was purple and the other blue. There was also a white, apron-like garment that Micah had told her would go over the dress. He'd also left her a white bonnet that he called a Kapp, and there was a pair of black boots at the foot of the bed, but Micah said if they were too big, it was acceptable to go barefoot. Apparently, shoes were optional except for church.

Church.

"If I get that far." Ruth took a deep breath. She'd already taken too long to change her clothes and expected a knock on the door at any moment to say the jig is up.

She walked over to the bed and quickly removed everything Englisch from her body and replaced it with things that were Amish. She circled the room, looking for a mirror, but came up empty. Another thing she would have to learn to do without. She would just have to hope that she looked the part if any of Micah's family showed up, because she had no way of seeing herself.

She'd done the best she could to secure the dress with the stickpins with which it was meant to be fastened, but both the dress and the white apron hung on her like sacks. She thought this interesting because Connie wasn't much bigger than her. Ruth figured she must be doing something wrong with the garments.

She picked up the little bonnet and put it on her head. Her long curls poked out from underneath it. Connie had pulled every strand of her own hair back into a tight bun, but Ruth didn't think her hair would do that. She wondered if she had to wear this Kapp or if she could go without it. *Connie won't even know I'm not wearing it,* Ruth figured and removed it. Maybe Micah could get a bigger size for her to use when she had to go out and about. For now, she held the Kapp in her hands and readied herself to head back out into the main part of the house.

Ruth pressed the dress down to smooth out any wrinkles, then quietly opened the door. She peeked out to see if she could spot Micah down the hall. He had apparently heard her, because he quickly stepped into her line of sight at the other end of the short corridor.

The two of them stood looking at each other in silence. She wished he would say that she looked just right, but he said nothing. She didn't want to give herself away in front of Connie, but she needed to know if she had done anything wrong. Connie wouldn't notice, but everyone else in the community would, and she wanted to know what she needed to do to correct any errors before that time came.

Tomorrow would be the day that Micah would take her to meet all of his family. Ruth didn't need a mirror to tell her that she probably didn't look like any of them. That had to be what Micah was thinking right now as he stared at her without saying a word. He had to be asking himself why he had ever thought this would work.

"I don't think it fits," she said. She held the Kapp up to him. "This definitely won't fit my head."

She moved out of the shadows closer to him and heard Connie's rocker in the back room. As she neared Micah, she saw a strange look in his eyes. It clearly wasn't a look of disappointment or concern, but she couldn't make out what his expression meant exactly.

He lifted his hand, and she thought he would take the Kapp, but instead, he pushed her curls behind her ear. "You have to hold these back. Then it will fit." His hand lingered behind her ear while his fingers twirled in her hair. "I wish it wasn't so," he whispered. "You have very pretty hair."

She reached up and touched his hand. As she held his fingers at her cheek, Micah turned and looked at the place where their hands touched. Then he brought both of their hands down and held her hand between them. The moment felt deeply personal, and Ruth knew that indulging in such intimacy was not a wise idea in their circumstances.

Ruth cleared her throat and whispered, "Does she suspect anything?"

Micah looked over his shoulder in the direction of the back room where his aunt had returned to. He shook his head. "She already loves you. Just as I thought." He said this with a frown. He sighed and closed his eyes for a moment. "I didn't expect to feel so guilty about this. I don't like lying."

Ruth didn't either, but they had already put this plan in motion, and she saw no way out of it now. "Help me do my hair so I look like everyone else."

Micah turned her around and pulled her hair back tighter than she had ever had it. She winced many times, and she wondered where he had learned to do this. "How many sisters do you have?" she asked.

"Five sisters and two brothers. As the oldest, I have a lot of experience doing this." He turned her around, and that strange look in his eyes came back. "For a moment there, I would have thought you had always been Amish." He reached for her Kapp and placed it gently on her head. "The strings hang down and rest on your apron. You don't have to tie them." He leaned close, touching his cheek to hers, and then whispered in her ear, "For the record, though, you don't look like everyone else."

The way he said it sent a shiver up Ruth's spine. She felt herself blush and looked down as he stepped back. "I just want to be sure I won't stand out," she said.

"Stand out? You'll stand out as the prettiest Amish girl in Lancaster County. Believe me."

Ruth knew she had to be bright red now. "You're just being nice," she said, but as he led her down the hallway, Ruth thought that perhaps she would be able to pull this off after all.

When they walked into the room, Aunt Connie turned in their direction. "Rachel, I would love to hear all about your move from out west. Are you originally from one of the Colorado communities? I have a dear friend in the community there. Perhaps you know Etta Miller. Is she a relative of yours?"

Ruth shot a glare at Micah. How quickly the conversation had become personal. At the shake of his head, she searched within her memory for the correct word. No . . . *nee*! "Nee," she said a bit too loud. "Nee," she repeated an octave lower.

"Ruth was born in Colorado, but she wasn't born Amish. More recently, she has lived in Washington. Up near Canada." Micah then explained further in a dialect Ruth had yet to figure out.

Connie's forehead creased. "*Ach*, that's too bad. I don't recall knowing anyone from that far distance." She lifted the knitting in her lap. "But that doesn't matter. You're here now, and we're glad to have you."

Ruth failed to remember the word for "thank you." She looked to Micah for a silent plea of help. As soon as he mouthed the word, she recalled it and shouted, "Danki!"

Micah cringed.

Connie chuckled. "Dear, I'm blind, not deaf."

How could she have been so careless? Ruth took a moment to begin again. She had a feeling the days ahead would have many restarts. But Connie was the only person who wouldn't see the horror on her face every time she messed up.

"I'm sorry," she said, then tried to remember the Amish words. She completely botched them into something not even close to correct.

Connie's fingers stilled over her knitting. She didn't look up, but the room became quiet. Micah covered his mouth. He appeared to be holding back a laugh. Ruth held her breath as she waited for Connie to accuse her of not being Amish.

Connie's fingers then began to move again over her project. "You two must be hungry after your long bus ride from Ohio. Feel free to use my kitchen to drum up a nice, hearty breakfast for yourselves. It will give Rachel time to . . . grow accustomed to cooking here."

"Danki, Aunt Connie," Micah said. Then he said something else in Pennsylvania Dutch that made no sense to Ruth. He turned and ushered Ruth out of the room and into the kitchen.

The kitchen appeared relatively modern. The appliances looked like those at her sister's place, though her limited knowledge of the Amish told her that none of them could run on electricity. She assumed gas, maybe? Natural sunlight streamed through large windows, filling the room with a warm glow that made her feel welcome. She knew, though, that her time here would likely be short. Especially since she'd slipped up so soon after meeting Connie. Judging by Micah's laugh, Ruth didn't want to know what she had really said to the woman.

"She knows, doesn't she?" Ruth whispered when they were alone by the stove. "I messed up already. I make the worst Amish person ever."

Micah's cheeks flushed red. He reached for a cast-iron pan from a hook above the stove. As it clattered down on the burner, he muttered something under his breath. Ruth couldn't be sure, but she thought he said something about being in trouble.

She had to agree. This whole setup spelled trouble with a capital *T*.

Micah cracked an egg into the hot pan, and the noise of its sizzle filled the room. He hoped it drowned out the sound of his beating heart. He feared that Ruth could hear it. He didn't know what had come over him, but the moment she walked out of her bedroom, his whole plan had shifted. His immediate thought was that he had never seen such a beautiful Amish woman in his life. He had to remind himself that she wasn't Amish at all, and that they weren't really engaged.

"I've never cooked over a flame before," Ruth whispered beside him. She was mere inches from him, and he could feel her soft breath against his cheek. She watched his every movement with rapt attention. The way she gnawed on her lower lip told him that she was worried about remembering how to work in an Amish kitchen. She glanced nervously at the icebox that would need fresh ice every day.

"In a few days, I'm sure you'll be fine." Micah spoke low to keep Aunt Connie from hearing. Speaking low also allowed him to stay close to Ruth. "I'll be here to help you learn."

Ruth nodded and offered a sweet smile. "First, I'd like you to show me how to tighten this dress." She turned around to give him access to her back.

Micah stared at the curve of her neck below her Kapp. Her skin looked creamy soft. He cleared his throat and put down the spatula. He reached out to touch the back of her apron but stopped an inch away. This task felt incredibly personal, even intimate.

"Aunt Connie would help you, for certain sure." His words came out in a way that made his throat sound clogged. Ruth glanced over her shoulder at him.

"She won't think it's weird that I don't know?" Panic filled her eyes.

"I don't know," Micah admitted, feeling just as worried. "I'll come up with some reason why you need her to show you. I just think it's best. I'll ask her for you after breakfast."

Ruth tilted her head. "Why would it be best?"

Micah swallowed hard as he searched for a valid response that didn't betray the whole truth. "It just wouldn't be appropriate."

Ruth sighed and rolled her eyes to the ceiling. "Will I ever get this right? I'm sorry. I'm just learning all of your rules. I'll remember that. No touching."

As soon as she said those words, he wished he hadn't said anything. He forced a smile, though, knowing it was just as well. In a few weeks they would both go their separate ways. Clearly he was attracted to her. But perhaps that attraction was nothing more than a response to all she was doing for him. Ruth was his path to his dream.

"Have I said 'thank you' yet?" he whispered.

She slowly turned back to face him. "For what?"

Her innocence captured his heart. She really had no idea what a key role her presence was playing. "For being a light in my life. It's like you've come along to guide me to where Gött wants me to be. I don't take your struggles lightly. Believe me, I know it's hard. I know how rules can crush a person."

Ruth's gaze narrowed, and for a moment Micah could almost feel the thread of understanding that linked them. "You get it." She placed her hand on his chest. Her touch was gentle, but he felt it to his core. "Our lives may look completely different, but we've had to bear similar weights. I'm just as grateful for you, Micah. We're going to get through this together." She looked at the refrigerator again. "Even if I do have to spend my mornings lugging ice." She giggled, and the musical sound touched him deeply.

The floor creaked behind them. "You two lovebirds better not be taking advantage of me," Aunt Connie said. "You're not married yet, and I may be blind, but I'm not a fool."

Micah stepped away from Ruth and looked down at the pan. The eggs were burned to a crisp. He suddenly realized that the smell had filled the house, and he hadn't even noticed.

"I'm sorry, Aunt Connie. I didn't mean to burn breakfast. I'll be more careful next time."

Connie chuckled. "I was young once and burned my share of meals. It's funny how easily the mind can become distracted. But today is pie day. Let's not burn them, shall we?"

Ruth backed away and went to stand at the other side of the counter as Connie opened a cabinet and brought out a bowl of apples. When Micah finally glanced Ruth's way, he saw that her eyes danced with silent laughter. She was such a joy. He felt immediate guilt for making her live the very strict life he was trying to run from. If she resented him for it, she didn't show it. In fact, as she and Connie set to peeling the apples for the pies, Ruth looked right at home in the Amish kitchen.

"They shall celebrate the fame of Your abundant goodness, Lord, and shall sing aloud of Your righteousness," Connie quoted the Psalm and then began to sing a hymn he knew well from the *Ausbund* church hymnal. He joined in on the next line just as Ruth reached for another apple.

She paused with her hand in the bowl and a smile on her face. As he finished the first verse, she gave him a nod of approval, and that was all the encouragement he needed to let go and sing with his whole heart.

Ruth Griffin was already setting him free, and they hadn't even left the community yet.

CHAPTER EIGHT

Micah stood at the end of the long lane that led to his family's farm. The hard dirt path followed a white fence all the way from the house to the road, passing by acres of farmland and horse pasture. The family had brought in the fall harvest before he left town, but the plow still stood out in the field. He'd have to bring it in, he assumed. His younger brother Paul was probably waiting for his help. There were a lot of other things that his family was waiting for him to do.

First and foremost, bring home a bride.

Before he'd left for Ohio, his *Mamm* had already been sterilizing the canning jars. She would be expecting another woman's help, given that she thought he'd be returning with Rachel. Micah was certain sure that Ruth wouldn't know how to can the garden's harvest. He had so much to explain to her in so little time. It was all so overwhelming if he stopped to think about it. But canning was the least of his concerns.

First, he needed to explain his early arrival to his parents.

The sun was beginning to set, so he knew dinner would soon be on the table. His family wouldn't be expecting him. He wondered when they would see him coming down the lane.

Alone.

He prepared for the barrage of questions that was sure to come. He was glad he'd decided to take Ruth to Connie's first. He needed time to set the stage before bringing Ruth with him. He knew their scrutiny of her would be fierce.

As he walked around a curve in the lane, he saw his oldest sister out back, behind the house, removing the bed linens from the clothesline. Sadie wasn't too far off from her own courting days, and he knew she would have her pick. Her Kapp had fallen on her back, and her blond hair glowed gold in the setting sun as she reached to unpin a pillowcase. She would make a *gut* Fraa. He considered going to his sister first. Breaking his news to one person didn't seem as daunting as breaking it to nine. She might even run in and break the news for him, saving him from having to find the right words. At least he hadn't returned empty-handed. That was much less humiliating than having to admit that the real Rachel Miller had rejected him. Before he could make up his mind, though, the front door on the wraparound porch opened, and his Daed, Jacob Stolzfus, stepped out with his brother Paul. Telling Sadie first wasn't an option now.

Micah made his way along the stepping-stones and up the eight stairs to the porch, stopping on the last one. Before they could open their mouths to ask any questions, he blurted out, "Rachel is staying with Aunt Connie. We decided to wait a little while before marrying, but she returned with me so we can have time to get to know each other." He held his breath as he waited for their response.

His words were met with dead silence.

Paul's blue eyes, so similar to Micah's, widened in shock. He let out a slow whistle and finally said in a singsong voice, "You're in trouble."

Daed tapped Paul on the shoulder and said, "See to your Mamm in the kitchen."

"Ach," Paul said. "That's women's work. I'd much rather stay out here and hear the reason for this."

"It's none of your concern," Daed told him.

Paul sputtered. "None of my concern? I'm twenty-two years old and ready to get married. But you've bought him a farm, and you haven't bought one for me. I deserve to hear his reason for putting marriage off again. Otherwise, give *me* the farm."

"Please, Paul." Daed placed his hand on his son's shoulder. "Your time will come."

Paul made a small huffing sound and shook his head, but he did as he was asked and left Micah and his father alone.

Daed was a big man: well over six feet tall with a long, bushy red beard. Threads of gray had recently started to dominate both his beard and dark hair. If stress was what brought on gray hair, Micah figured he had contributed to both his parents' outward aging. He waited for his Daed to tell him how he had once again disappointed his family.

"Daed, this was Rachel's idea," Micah spoke first. "She didn't want to get married . . . yet." This wasn't a *total* lie. "What was I supposed to do? Leave her?"

"I'll tell you what you should have done." His father spoke low so Micah had to lean in to hear him. "You should have stayed on and courted her. Think about what you've done now. You've taken an unmarried Amish girl across state lines with no chaperone. I'm surprised her parents allowed it."

Micah felt his stomach churn as his mother stepped out the front door to join them. Leah Stolzfus had black hair like Micah and the same blue eyes as her sons. "Paul told me you returned without being married. What's this all about?"

Micah stood on the top step looking up at his parents and feeling small. He'd known that they wouldn't be happy that they'd traveled unchaperoned. But he and Ruth had had no choice, and now it was time to face the music. "We were on a bus with many people. I suppose I thought since we weren't alone, it would be fine. She's staying with Aunt Connie."

His Mamm wrung her hands in her apron. "I knew this wasn't going to work. Elder Joseph said he didn't know these people and could only go by their bishop's recommendation. We should have gone there ourselves to meet the family. But we couldn't leave the little children, especially Daisy. Why, Micah? Why do we keep coming back to being at square one with you? It's time to grow up."

Micah hated seeing his mother distraught, especially knowing that he was the cause of her distress once again. How many times had he let his parents down? He stepped up and reached for her hands. Whereas his father was robust, his mother was petite and only came to Micah's shoulder. He'd definitely caused the worry lines on her face. She'd probably develop many more lines once he left forever.

"Mamm, there will still be a wedding. Rachel just needs time. Once you meet her, you'll see how shy she is."

"This week," she said with a stern face. "The wedding must happen this week, for certain sure. Bishop Yoder can hold the ceremony here in two days. A Saturday night ceremony will be fine. If her parents hoped to attend, then they should have made sure it happened in Ohio, as planned."

Micah swallowed hard. *Two days?*

His heart started beating fast. There couldn't be a wedding. Ruth would never go for such a thing. If his parents pushed ahead with this plan, it would ruin everything. Micah did his best to keep his panic from showing on his face. Why hadn't he anticipated that they would require this of them?

"Please, meet Rachel first before you put this expectation on her. She needs time to get used to the idea of marriage, not to mention getting used to me. Her parents forced her to do this." *Just like mine did,* he thought. "I'm sure once she gets to know everyone, she'll be more comfortable with the idea."

His parents looked at each other, and then his mother nodded at Micah.

"There is no church service this Sunday," Micah's father said, "but you will go see Elder Joseph first thing tomorrow to ask for forgiveness. You will do as he says so you might be reconciled. If he requires you to marry Rachel quickly, you will. The decision will be out of our hands. Is that understood?"

Micah hesitated. He was in no position to make such a declaration. Ruth would probably run away if she even overheard this conversation. Whatever he had to do to convince Elder Joseph to give her time, Micah would do it.

"I expect to see Rachel here tomorrow for dinner," Mamm said. "I appreciate that she's staying at my sister's. But the only way for her to feel comfortable around us is to make sure she is here every day."

"I can bring over the extra buggy for her to use so she doesn't have to walk every day," Daed suggested.

Micah bit back a smile as he imagined what Ruth would think of driving a buggy. "If it's acceptable, I would like to escort her each day back and forth. I am, after all, courting her."

His parents looked at each other again. "In the open buggy only," Mamm said at last.

Micah felt better with this arrangement. Now he only had to convince Elder Joseph to forgive him. He didn't want to think of the disaster that would ensue if the elder required a quick wedding of them. If that was the case, Micah figured there was a good chance that tomorrow he would be leaving town for good.

"It will be dinner soon, so it's time to make bread," Connie said. She bustled around her kitchen, reaching for the flour, water, and yeast.

"You're very independent," Ruth observed.

"For certain sure. I lost my eyesight when I was a teenager from a bacterial infection. After that, my parents sent me to a school for the blind. There was no pity party there." Connie measured out all her ingredients using cups and spoons she seemed to recognize by feel. She kept her face lifted as if she was staring off at something on the wall behind Ruth.

"Can you see anything at all?" Ruth pressed her lips tight, wondering if she'd just said something offensive. "I'm sorry. You don't have to answer that. I don't want to be rude."

"Don't be silly. If we're going to live together for a time, you should know my capabilities and understand where I might need some help. I've mostly learned how to get along, and my sister and her children stop over quite regularly and help with cleaning places I might've missed." Connie smiled and winked. Her sunny disposition amazed Ruth. Her independence was impressive.

"How long have you lived alone?"

"Since I returned from the school. I was twenty-one years old. I very nearly stayed on permanently." Connie frowned as her fingers folded the dough and kneaded it to completion. "But that's another story," she said, efficiently ending that line of questioning.

Ruth felt badly. "Forgive me. I've never met a blind person, and I fear I've overstepped my bounds."

"You didn't say anything wrong," Connie said quietly. "I'm here to help you find your way in our community. There are just some things from my past that still hurt. But you don't need to be worrying about an old lady and her bygone days." She placed the dough into a pan and carried it to the counter. Then she opened the oven and, feeling the raised dots on top of the braille thermometer, said, "Right on schedule. The roast should be ready in a little over an hour."

"It's amazing that you can tell," Ruth exclaimed. Connie impressed her deeply. "And by the way, you're *not* old. You can't even be near fifty."

Connie's eyes were now twinkling again, and she smirked. "Almost, but not quite." She turned in the direction of the rising dough. "We'll give that an hour to proof. The oven is making it quite toasty in here, which should speed the rising process along." She felt her way toward the kitchen table and took the chair beside Ruth. "Let's chat, shall we?"

Suddenly, Ruth felt a little uneasy. Connie reached over and took her hand and gave it a squeeze. "I understand that your parents arranged your marriage to Micah. I also understand why you chose not to marry him right away. It is wise to get to know a man before you spend your life with him." She frowned, and Ruth remembered what Micah had told her about a man having previously been in Connie's life.

"I hope you don't mind me saying so, but Micah told me that you once had someone you loved too. But he said it didn't work out."

Connie sighed and leaned back in her chair. "Ja, but that was years ago. He was blind as well, and his parents feared that it wouldn't be wise for him to marry another blind person." She looked around her kitchen as if she could see everything around her. "I think I've proven that we would have been fine. Maybe proving that is still what drives me daily to get up and keep putting one foot in front of the other. But life alone wasn't always so smooth. It took me years to learn to get through my day on my own." She laughed aloud. "I even had to learn to put on a dress all over again."

Ruth thought of the way her own dress hung on her like a potato sack. Micah had told her he would ask Connie how to put it on and pin it right. She'd thought it strange that he would suggest that when they were trying to pass her off as Amish. A twenty-one-year-old Amish girl would know how to put on a dress.

Connie stood up and, pushing her chair back, said, "I had to learn by feeling my way." She reached behind her back for something, and when she brought her hands to the front, Ruth saw that the dress pins were in her hands. Connie placed them on the table and turned sideways. "I learned how to find the pleat and to cinch back here with my fingers." She grabbed a pin and slipped it effortlessly into the fabric, to hold it in place. She did the same for the other side as Ruth watched with rapt attention. A moment later, Connie stood in front of her with her dress once again secured correctly.

Ruth felt behind her for her pins and tried to copy Connie's movements. It was almost as if Connie knew she needed to learn how to dress herself correctly. Ruth shook the idea off. Connie couldn't see her. She couldn't possibly know that Ruth had struggled with the dress.

Could she?

A strange thought occurred to her: was Connie pretending to be blind, just like Ruth was pretending to be Rachel?

Nee, Ruth thought to herself. She nearly laughed out loud when she realized she'd automatically thought the Amish word for no.

She looked at Micah's aunt again. No, she was sure that Connie wasn't pretending to be physically blind. But perhaps Connie could see in different ways.

"Are you nervous about meeting Micah's family tomorrow?" Connie took her seat again.

"How did you know?" Ruth asked.

"Who wouldn't be? But let me assure you that my sister and her brood are a loving family. They're excited to finally have Micah married. He's given them some worries these past few years. They bought him a farm, which I'm sure he told you."

Ruth wasn't going to say anything at first. But then she thought she might be able to use the moment to help her friend. "Connie," she asked, "what if someone doesn't want to be a farmer?"

Connie tilted her head. "There are a few other trades, but Micah has never wanted to do one of those. He's farmed his whole life. It's all he knows."

That and music, Ruth thought to herself.

"He has a beautiful voice," Ruth approached the conversation warily. "Don't you think?"

Connie shrugged. "I suppose."

"Have you ever told him so?"

"Nee," Connie said. "Compliments can lead to pride, and that is not our way."

The kitchen instantly felt very warm to Ruth. When she touched her neck, she could feel perspiration on it. Silence settled around her and Connie as she realized that she had just broken one of the rules. The Amish avoided entertainment not because entertainment was bad, necessarily, but because it led to pride. Suddenly she realized Micah's dilemma. If he sought out a career in music, others would think he considered himself higher than the people in his community.

But what if music was what made him happy? Surely, they wanted him to be happy.

Then again, she thought, *maybe they don't consider his happiness their concern.*

"My dear, is there something we should know?" Connie grabbed her hand again, but this time the gesture didn't feel as welcoming as before.

"I just want to know how to make him happy," Ruth said carefully. "I honestly don't know him well enough to know what that might take."

Connie smiled. "Ach, you will have years to figure that out. He's clearly already smitten with you. You should've heard the way he talked about you when you were getting settled in your room. Rachel this, and Rachel that. I would say you've already made him quite happy."

Ruth nodded, knowing that was true. Just a few hours before, in this very kitchen, he'd thanked her for all she was doing for him. How sad it was that his family didn't see what would really make him happy. It was even sadder that he would have to leave his loved ones behind forever to find that happiness.

Connie had assured her that Micah's family would love her. But given what she knew, she wondered if she could love *them*.

She supposed that tomorrow she would find out.

CHAPTER NINE

Micah drove his open-air buggy down the lane toward his family's home. He had picked up Ruth to bring her to Friday night dinner, but they had been driving for a while, and she hadn't said a word in twenty minutes, since the last two turns in the road. The way she held the bottom of her seat in a white-knuckled grip told him she was just as nervous as he was.

"You'll fit right in," he assured her. Anyone passing by would have no idea that she hadn't spent her whole life in the Amish community. She even wore a demure expression that gave an impression of innocence and faith. He was pleased to see her hair properly pulled back, though he missed the curls that used to frame her face. He hadn't initially noticed that her face was heart-shaped, as her curls had masked this feature. When he found himself yearning to see her long hair around her shoulders again, he reminded himself that would never be possible. Unless . . .

Micah cleared his throat and looked out into the pasture. He could see his brother coming their way. A coil of rope hung from Paul's shoulder, and when he reached the fence, he tossed it over a post. Next, he leaped sideways over the fence. Then he wiped his hands on his pants, beamed, and headed in their direction.

"That's my brother," Micah told Ruth. "I would say he's the happiest of them all that I'm getting married . . . or supposedly getting married."

"Why is he happy about it?" Ruth finally spoke. Her mind had appeared to be elsewhere.

"My father said he has to wait to get married until after me. I said Paul shouldn't have to wait, but Daed has his own ideas about things." Micah brought the buggy to a halt with a "Whoa."

"Hello," Paul said to Ruth in English. He didn't even look at Micah. "I'm Paul."

Ruth put a smile on her face and said, "I'm Rachel. It's nice to meet you" in the Amish dialect.

Micah glanced her way, surprised at how perfectly the Pennsylvania Dutch came out. She had obviously been practicing and had caught on quickly. But he knew she couldn't know too much more of their language yet.

Paul looked at Micah for the first time. "My *Bruder* said you felt more comfortable with English, but you sound fine to me."

Ruth replied, "I appreciate you all speaking English to me, as it does come easier. Pennsylvania Dutch wasn't my first language."

Paul eyed her with a nod. "That's what Micah said." Then he said in dialect, "Where are you from again?"

Ruth froze beside Micah. Leave it to his brother to test her.

Micah said, "Colorado. Then Washington before her family moved to Ohio and became Amish." He reached for her hand and gave it a quick squeeze. "Rachel is quite shy. She'll warm up to everyone soon, for certain sure. Right, Rachel?"

As if on cue, a blush spread across her cheeks, and she dropped her head to his shoulder. "It does take me a little bit to feel comfortable. Thank you for understanding, Paul."

Paul glanced at them both for an elongated minute while he chewed on the inside of his cheek. "Of course. I suppose that's why you needed extra time before getting married?"

She nodded demurely. "I was so grateful for Micah's understanding."

"I just hope it doesn't take too long." Paul's voice was gruff.

Micah sent his brother a warning look not to cross that boundary, but Paul either missed it or ignored it, because he asked, "Are you the oldest in your family? Are there others waiting to get married too?"

Micah could feel Ruth tense up beside him. He knew she did not know how to answer. He had neglected to tell Ruth about Rachel's familial status. But he couldn't let her sit there in silence either. That would only make his brother even more curious.

"Paul, can we save this conversation for when everyone's around? No sense in making her give the same answers over and over again."

Paul glanced from him to Ruth and back, then shrugged. "Ja, for certain sure. I look forward to hearing all she has to say." He walked away, back to his rope, and Micah continued to drive down the lane. A minute later, he pulled the buggy up into the barn and locked the brakes.

"Okay, I'd guess that we have maybe five minutes before we get bombarded by my very large family. Rachel is the second-oldest child of the Miller family. She has three brothers that are younger than her and one older sister who is already married. I'm sorry I neglected to tell you that."

Ruth let out a deep breath. "I hope they don't ask me anything else I don't know."

"Don't worry if they do. They don't know Rachel at all. So anything you tell them isn't going to be fact-checked right away. They'll take you at your word for tonight. By the time they figure out the truth, we should both be long gone."

She gave her knees a little pat, as if bracing herself. "All right," she said. "Let's do this." She hopped down off the buggy just as Sadie and Daisy came into the barn.

Micah's oldest sister carried the younger girl on her hip. Though Daisy was nine years old, she was small in stature as a result of the disability she'd had her whole life. The brace she wore on her leg provided support, but walking was still difficult for her.

"Welcome back, Bruder," Sadie said, but she didn't look at Micah at all. Both girls had their eyes on Ruth. Excitement over meeting their soon-to-be sister showed on their faces. "It's nice to meet you, Rachel." Sadie spoke in Pennsylvania Dutch.

"Danki." Ruth dropped her gaze and nodded. "Same to you," she added in English.

Sadie tilted her head in question, then said, "I forgot to speak English."

Daisy was struggling to get down, and this distraction seemed to keep her from asking why Ruth wanted to speak English. Daisy walked slowly toward Ruth, and Ruth stepped up to meet her halfway. Ruth knelt down so that they were eye to eye.

Daisy reached for Ruth's face and cupped her cheeks in her hands. "You're so pretty. I'm so happy to meet you," she said in Pennsylvania Dutch. The little girl's red braids hung against the front of her dress. Her little white Kapp fit snugly on her head, and the strings waived with her braids when she tilted her head at Ruth.

Ruth glanced over to Micah for a translation, but his throat clogged. "Rachel is happy to meet all of you as well." He left it at that. "Shall we head in? I'm sure Daed and Mamm are eager to meet Rachel too."

The first opportunity for questioning had passed. As they walked inside, Sadie held the kitchen door wide for everyone to go through. Micah was the last in line, and she put her hand out to stop him.

"Give her time to get used to everybody," he said quietly before she could say anything.

Sadie frowned and kept her hand on his sleeve. "I'm more concerned about you, Bruder. Just be sure about what you are doing."

Micah was taken aback by this show of concern. He had expected questions from Sadie and maybe even a rebuke.

He touched Sadie's hand and said, "I am." Indeed, he was sure Ruth was his ticket out of Lititz. He looked over and saw that his mother was already holding Ruth in an embrace by the kitchen table. He watched as Ruth wrapped her arms around his Mamm and held on for a long moment. Suddenly, he wasn't sure about anything. He had been worried that bringing Ruth here was a bad idea because his family would not accept her.

Perhaps he should have been more afraid that they would.

"How is my sister?" Leah Stolzfus asked Ruth. Thankfully, she spoke in English. Over her shoulder, Ruth could see Paul staring at them with an inquisitive expression, but she was glad everyone else was accepting of the request.

"*Gut.*" Ruth looked around the large room, which appeared to serve as both the kitchen and living room. Ruth had never seen a room so big, but the family of ten seemed to fit comfortably in the space. The last rays of daylight beamed in brightly through the large windows. "She's been a wonderful hostess. I'm so blessed to be staying with her."

"Wunderbaar. And we are so blessed to have you with us." Leah stepped back and held Ruth's hands. The woman wore a warm smile on her face, which looked so much like her son's.

Ruth realized that she was holding her breath. The whole scene felt like a dream. How long had it been since her own mother had looked at her like this? Ruth had forgotten what it felt like to be held so lovingly.

"Komm, sit and tell us about yourself," Leah said.

Micah stepped up behind Ruth and pulled out a chair for her to take. Ruth smiled at him. "Danki. You are all so kind." As soon as she sat, Micah's family surrounded her.

Ruth could feel her face flush under the gaze of ten pairs of eyes. Everyone was waiting to see what she would say and do. She looked up to find Micah beside her. When he placed his hand on her shoulder, she reached for it, and their fingers entwined. Immediately, Ruth felt right at home.

"Rachel is still a bit tired from her journey," Micah said. "Maybe we could talk about her life after dinner?"

Ruth looked up at him, wondering why he wanted to delay the inevitable. Deciding that he must have his reasons, she followed his lead. "What he says is true. If you don't mind, I would love to hear a little bit about each of you while we have dinner."

A little boy who couldn't be more than seven said, "You sound funny." He eyed her suspiciously. Ruth knew that he was only voicing what everyone else in the room thought. Children seldom held back their thoughts.

Micah said, "Rachel is from Ohio."

Ruth squeezed his fingers tight. "Actually, I'm from Colorado originally. We moved to Washington State before Ohio. Did you forget already, Micah?" The two of them needed to stay on their chosen storylines. One wrong slip and things could go badly for Micah. And for her, if she lost her housing. She knew she needed to start looking around for someplace else to go. Surely this charade could only last a couple of weeks at best. As she looked back at all the people staring at her, she wondered if it would even last that long.

"Rachel, would you help me with the stew?"

Ruth looked around the table to see who would answer, and they all stared back at her. Suddenly she realized Leah was talking to her. *She* was Rachel. How could she have forgotten something so simple as her name?

"I'm sorry. Ja, of course, I can help you." She pushed back in her chair to stand. "It smells wonderful. And is that apple pie?" Two pies sat under the windowsill on a side table next to the counter.

"Ja. The apples are right from our own orchard." Leah led Ruth toward a bowl of batter on the counter. "The dumplings will need to be made and dropped into the pot."

A big pot simmered over a flame on the stove. Ruth approached the stove carefully. She also had no idea how to make dumplings. She stared at the contents in the bowl. "Do I have to do anything else, or are these ready to go?"

Leah passed over two oven mitts. "Put these on before you lift the lid of the pot so you don't burn yourself. The batter is ready."

Ruth put the mitts on and moved toward the stove. But as she attempted to lift the lid with one hand, the tip of her other oven mitt caught the fire beneath. Suddenly, it went up in flames on her hand. Not knowing what to do, especially in a kitchen with no running water, Ruth stood there in shock.

Leah rushed over and moved her toward a basin. She lifted a jug and poured water into it. "Drop it in here, quick!"

Ruth did as she was told, and Leah had the fire out right away.

"Ach! How about you set the table instead?"

Ruth nodded. She still felt on edge after what had just happened. "I think that would be a *gut* idea."

But when she reached the table, she realized that she had no idea how an Amish table was set. She tentatively touched the utensils and started to put them out on the table. Glancing around, she saw a few of the kids watching her every move.

"I'm not sure how you want me to do this," she admitted. A few giggles followed.

Leah shushed her children. "Sadie, why don't you help her?"

Sadie rolled her eyes and folded her arms. "I want to see how she does it first."

"That is not how we welcome our guest," Leah scolded her daughter. She pressed her lips tight for a moment before looking at Ruth. "On second thought, why don't you take Daisy out and play by the garden with her? I think that would be best for tonight. You're a guest, and we shouldn't expect you to perform chores on your first evening." She gave her other children stern looks. "The rest of you get moving on your tasks. I'll talk to you in a little while about your behavior."

The tension in the room was so thick, Ruth felt like she could cut it with the knife in her hand. She placed the knife on the table and looked to Daisy. Suddenly she wanted nothing more than to get out of the house that had felt so welcoming just a few moments before.

"I would love to take Daisy out." Ruth looked at the young child. "Would you like that? Perhaps we can go for a walk."

The little girl looked around at her older brothers and sisters as if to see if they approved of this plan. She shrugged.

Micah said, "It's okay, Daisy. Go with Rachel."

The little girl nodded. She lifted her hand to Ruth, and the two of them headed toward the door. Daisy moved slowly because of her brace.

Ruth would have loved to run from the room. So strong was her desire to escape, she nearly scooped the child up to carry her outside. Instead, she forced herself to walk patiently beside Daisy. She tried to ignore the feeling of all those eyes boring into her back. If she had thought for a moment that the others had accepted her, that feeling was gone now.

The little girl led her outside onto the porch and down a set of stairs. No sound came from the kitchen behind the screen door. Not until Ruth reached the garden. Then she could hear loud voices streaming out all the windows, all at once.

The most common phrase she heard was "Nee Amish."

CHAPTER TEN

"Do you want me to take her back?" Micah asked. The others' faces betrayed their shock at the bride he'd brought home. "Let's not forget this was your idea." He had been working so hard to make sure Ruth passed the initial inspection, it hadn't occurred to him that his parents might actually change their minds. Perhaps he could be freed of this marriage right away.

"Did you speak to Elder Joseph?" Daed asked.

Micah hesitated. Or maybe this would be harder than he thought. "Ja?" he said uncertainly. He wondered where his father was going with this line of questioning.

"And what did he tell you? Has this girl been compromised by you traveling together?"

Micah's shoulders slumped as he remembered the meeting he'd had with the elder that morning. He leaned back into his chair and tapped his hands on the tabletop. His father sat at the head, and his mother sat on the other end. His siblings filled the other chairs along the table. The scrutiny was unbearable. He was the oldest, and he knew they were all watching to see what would happen in this situation. His parents had reminded him more times than he could count that he was the role model for them all.

"He's giving me a few weeks, but he expects a wedding soon." Micah's response sounded deflated even to his ears. The original plan would move forward.

And quickly.

Mamm nodded once. "Then we must figure out a way to accept this young woman as she is. If Elder Joseph respects the community she came from, then I will trust his judgment. We know she wasn't born Amish, but if that community accepted her family in, then I will do my best to do the same." She sighed and frowned. "I wondered why she had been passed by the young men of her own community. Well, so be it." She stood and walked back to the stove and her cooking.

One by one, Micah's siblings departed from the kitchen to return to their own chores before the meal. His father stood, too, and headed out to the barn. When Micah finally lifted his head, the only person left staring at him was Paul. Micah's parents appeared to have resolved themselves to the situation, but he could see that his brother had not.

Paul was standing a few feet away with his arms folded across his chest. "This whole thing doesn't feel right."

Micah had no desire to spar with his brother. "Rachel was not ready to get married," he said carefully. That part, at least, was the truth. "Coming here was the best choice we could make at the time. Can you at least give her a chance?" Micah saw his mother turn toward them from the stove.

"It's the least we can do," she said. "We did begin this, and we should see it through."

Paul clenched his jaw and shook his head. A minute later, he pushed the screen door wide and walked out onto the porch. Micah could hear him clumping down the steps to go help their father in the barn.

Mamm turned back to the stove to attend to the dumplings. Only the click of her metal spoon on the pot broke the silence in the room. Finally, she put her spoon down on the counter and turned to Micah. "Be patient with Paul. In his youth, he doesn't understand that sometimes time is a blessing." She wiped her hands on her apron and looked out the window toward the garden where Ruth and Daisy sat by the tomatoes. Mamm smiled slightly and said, "Rachel seems like she has a gentle heart. I like that." She looked Micah's way. "She will make a *gut* Fraa."

Micah swallowed hard and nodded. It was true. Ruth *would* make a wonderful wife one day.

Just not his.

Daisy may have been small in stature, Ruth quickly saw, but her mind was developed far beyond her years. Ruth tried to remember if she'd ever been as bold as this child. Even at twenty-one, Ruth doubted she could be so brave as Daisy was at nine.

The two of them sat over by the rows of tomato plants. Most of the garden had been harvested already, and from where she sat, Ruth could see batches of onions hanging from the porch ceiling, still covered in dirt.

"How long will the onions have to hang?" she asked the child.

Daisy shrugged. "I picked them two days ago. They have to stay in the open air but in the shade. I would say they'll still be there for about five weeks. Don't worry, we'll take them down for your wedding and then put them back."

A wave of guilt came over Ruth. She nodded, but her throat closed at the mention of the wedding. Pretending to be engaged had sounded hard enough at the time. It was even harder now that she had to lie to an innocent child. She turned her attention back to the garden. "You have an overabundance of tomatoes. You all must love them."

There were more rows of the plants than she could count.

Daisy snickered. "You must be *verdoddled*."

Ruth tilted her head at the word. She didn't know what it meant, but it didn't sound good. "Maybe?"

Daisy giggled again. "That's all right. I suppose everyone gets mixed up sometimes. We don't eat all those tomatoes all at once. We grow enough to last through the winter. Mamm makes juice and sauce, and sometimes she just leaves them whole in the jar. She also sells them at the market. If you're going to be a farmer's wife, you'd better learn all this."

Ruth nodded. "I suppose you're right. Perhaps I can join her when she goes."

Daisy moved a little closer. Seeing that she was struggling, Ruth scooted over to meet her halfway. Daisy leaned in as if she was going to share a secret. "Are you sure about marrying my brother?" Her eyes were round with curiosity.

"Um . . . this seems like a big conversation for someone your age," Ruth said. "How about you tell me about your school instead? How long have you been learning English? You speak so well."

Daisy went on as if she hadn't heard Ruth. "I love my brother. Do you?"

Ruth looked around to see if anyone had heard. She felt uncomfortable with the direction this conversation was going. "Well, as you know, we just met. So, to be honest, no, I don't love your brother. That's why we're taking time to get to know each other."

"That tells me that you're not good enough for him." Daisy planted her two fists on her hips, daring Ruth to deny the truth of her words.

Once again, Ruth felt envious of this child's boldness. "Micah is lucky to have someone like you in his corner. I don't think I've ever had anyone stick up for me quite like this." She didn't think she'd ever stuck up for *herself* quite like this. "I do care about your brother, and I would never want to do anything to hurt him. In fact, I want the best for him."

Ruth felt a little strange explaining this complicated situation to a nine-year-old, but Daisy seemed mature beyond her years. Perhaps her disability had forced her to grow up extra fast. Ruth wanted to ask Daisy about her brace, but the child spoke first.

"You can't marry Micah," Daisy said in a low, serious tone.

Once again, Ruth glanced around to see if anyone else was in earshot. She didn't see anyone else in the farmyard or gardens, and the house was too far away for Daisy's words to have carried.

Ruth cleared her throat and lowered her own voice. "Why's that?"

Daisy pursed her lips. She appeared to be deciding whether to say more. "You don't really know him," she said finally. "You don't know what makes him happy."

Ruth bit back a smile. She felt pretty sure she knew more about what made Micah happy than this child did. But then she remembered something Micah had said on their bus ride. He had mentioned that his little sister knew about his love for music.

"Do you know what makes him happy?" Ruth asked, testing the waters. She had to be careful. The risk was great if she mentioned Micah's talent to Daisy and then the girl told her parents.

Daisy nodded and glanced at the house. "It's a secret."

Ruth began to relax. She now felt that she had a confidant in Daisy. Still, she weighed her words carefully, just in case she was wrong. "I heard your brother sing at Aunt Connie's," she confessed. "He has a strong voice." Ruth hoped a strong voice wasn't considered something bad. She thought it a better word than *beautiful*, even though his voice was that too. But she didn't want it to sound like she was elevating Micah above the others in his community. Daisy's wide eyes told Ruth she was steering this conversation in the right direction.

"He let you hear him?" Daisy said in astonishment.

"Why? Does he not let people hear him sing?"

Daisy leaned close. "Just me and Aunt Connie. Mamm and Daed forbid it. They think he doesn't sing to worship Gött, but himself."

Ruth took in a sharp breath. It came to her that Micah must feel silenced in his own home. First, he had been misunderstood. Then his faith had been questioned too?

"Daisy, do you ever think it's possible that his singing could be a gift from Gött, and by not singing, he's not using his talent?"

"Ja, that's why you can't marry him. If you do, then he will never sing again."

More than anything, Ruth wanted to tell Daisy the truth. But if Micah wanted the girl to know about their plan, he would have to be the one to tell her.

"I can't say what the future will be," she said gently. "But I can tell you that I will always encourage Micah to follow his dreams, and if that means singing, then he must sing."

Daisy tilted her head at Ruth. "But he can't marry and follow his dream. It's why he hasn't married before this. So many girls wanted him to court them! It was sickening." Daisy's lips curled in youthful revulsion.

Ruth bit back a smile. "Yuck."

Daisy nodded twice. "Yuck, for certain sure." She squinted at Ruth. "You seem smart, Rachel. If I were you, I would go home before getting too attached to my Bruder."

Ruth stared over the child's Kapp to the sunset that was burning the sky a purplish hue. "I think I understand what you're saying." She dropped her gaze to her hands, which were folded in her lap. "Micah's real love will always be music, and he has no room in his life for a Fraa."

"Ja."

"Has he told his parents this?"

"Ja. That's when they got Elder Joseph involved and arranged his marriage. They said they needed to stop this nonsense."

"They think he's verdoddled," Ruth added, getting the swing of the language.

Daisy giggled. "But they're wrong. Lots of people will hear Micah sing someday."

It was clear to Ruth now that Daisy knew about Micah's plans on leaving the Amish. She thought it very sad that his only support was a nine-year-old child. But did Daisy understand the gravity of the situation?

Ruth took Daisy's hand in hers. "Sweetie, do you know what would happen if Micah went out there to become a singer? Do you know what would happen here?"

Daisy bit her lower lip and grew quiet. "I suppose Mamm and Daed would be mad. But once he was famous, they would be happy. Wouldn't they?"

Daisy may have been courageous beyond her years, but she was still a child. Ruth didn't want to be the one to tell her that if Micah's plan worked, Daisy would never see her brother again. Nor did she want to explain that Daisy's parents would be brokenhearted and that the community would have to forget Micah ever existed.

"Do you know any Amish families that had a family member leave to go become Englisch?"

Daisy shot her head up. "Micah's not going to become Englisch. He'll still be Amish."

Ruth wanted to say more, but she couldn't risk stirring things up so much that Daisy would go to her parents. Though it sounded to her like his parents already knew what Micah wanted and were doing everything in their power to set a different course for his life.

They had even bought him a farm.

Mamm and Daed Stolzfus were doing their best to arrange more than just a marriage for Micah. They were arranging his whole Amish life.

But why?

Ruth wondered what she was missing. There had to be a valid reason for their actions, and those actions had to be about more than just their fear of losing Micah to the Englisch world. After all, wouldn't they want their son to be happy, even if that meant letting him go?

Ruth saw Micah's father and Paul coming out of the barn. They closed the doors behind them and headed back toward the house just as Micah's mother stepped out onto the porch and announced dinner was ready.

Siblings came running from all directions. Micah came from around the front of the house and, instead of walking toward the kitchen door, headed their way.

As he drew close, he said, "What are my two favorite people talking about?"

Daisy frowned and said, "Rachel says you're—"

Ruth interrupted, "You're a strong singer, and I was hoping to hear you sing again someday soon. I'm so glad you have Daisy to share your dreams with."

Micah glanced at the house. Everyone had gone in now. He looked back at them and put his finger to his lips. "I will sing later, but it will be our little secret, right, Daisy? It has to be a secret." He scooped up his sister, and from over her head, he mouthed to Ruth, "For now."

He headed toward the house, chatting lovingly with his little sister. Ruth fell back and followed at a distance. She wondered if even Micah understood the gravity of the situation. She suddenly imagined him standing on the outskirts of the farm, looking back at the life he was walking away from.

Somehow, in her imagination, he didn't look happy. It occurred to her that, perhaps—even if he left Lititz and got the opportunity to sing—Micah would never be truly happy if he left his family behind.

And maybe his parents knew it.

CHAPTER ELEVEN

Monday morning was laundry day in the community, and Micah had brought Ruth over to his family's home to experience another day in their Amish life. There had been no community church this Sunday, for which Micah felt grateful. He wasn't up to introducing her to everyone else just yet. Ruth could only handle so much while growing accustomed to his simple life. Though, as he watched her struggle with hanging the laundry with Sadie, it occurred to him that she probably didn't think any of this was simple.

Sadie followed behind Ruth, adjusting every piece of clothing after Ruth hung it. Micah had always believed that there was something beautiful in the precise order of an Amish clothesline. Towels of various colors lined up one after another, all of them the same length. Sheets too. Next came dresses, followed by pants. It went this way all the way down the row, ending with the smallest of items—the socks. Each sock hung at the same exact length as the one beside it. Each toe pointed in the same direction. Because the Stolzfus family was so large, their clothesline extended from the porch all the way to the barn. Ruth and Sadie stood on the porch together, working side by side. Micah had never wanted to do laundry so badly before.

Daisy came out onto the back porch and caught sight of him. Her smile invited him over, giving him an excuse to leave his farmwork behind.

As he neared the porch, Sadie said, "Don't you come near my clean clothes, Bruder. Not with hands like that."

Micah looked down and swiped his filthy hands across his pant legs. He made a beeline for the watering hose. As the clean, cold water washed away the dirt on his hands, he glanced up and saw Ruth watching him.

"Scrub them," Sadie called, jolting Micah's attention away from the beguiling expression on Ruth's face. He wondered how long he had been staring. The numbness of his hands told him it was an amount of time that would probably be considered inappropriate. But as far as his family knew, he and Ruth were courting. They would think it totally appropriate for a couple preparing to be married to be enamored with each other. Only he and Ruth knew that was not the case, and yet . . . the hold she'd had on him a moment before had felt completely natural.

Micah turned the water off at the spigot and made his way to the porch steps. "Can I help with the laundry?"

Sadie made a scoffing sound. "That's so like you, Micah: showing up to offer aid when we're all finished. Maybe Rachel needs some help gathering the last of the tomatoes."

Micah looked at Ruth. She picked up a garden basket and reached for Daisy's hand.

"I don't need any help, but thank you. Us girls have it all under control, don't we?" Ruth offered Daisy the sweetest smile, piquing a bit of jealousy within him. He wished she'd smile at him.

As Ruth and Daisy descended the steps together, he could see that they were already forming a close bond. He should be happy to see a friendship blooming between them, but he knew that this probably wasn't a good idea. Daisy wouldn't understand when Ruth left in a few weeks. Then again, she would be even more hurt when *he* left.

Am I doing the right thing? he wondered.

Ja, he told himself. He had to make his escape to Nashville. If he didn't, he'd never be content.

"You're sweet on her already," Sadie said in a singsong voice when Ruth was out of earshot.

Micah glanced his sister's way, meaning to deny her words, but the heat scorching his face surely betrayed him. He pressed his lips tight. There was no point in denying his growing feelings for Ruth.

"She's an amazing person." He spoke the truth. "There's so much you don't know about her. You have only had her here on the farm a couple days. You haven't seen her selflessness the way I have."

"For certain sure I have," Sadie said. "She's meek but strong. And smart. Oh, so smart. The German language is taking root fast in her. It won't be long, and she'll be understanding everything we're saying. We won't be able to gossip about her right in front of her anymore."

"Gossip?" Micah raised his voice.

Sadie punched his shoulder. "Kidding, Bruder. Calm down. There is nothing bad I could say about your girl. I so hope she decides to marry you. I would love to have a sister so close to my age. You're right, Rachel is amazing."

Micah averted his gaze from Sadie's and searched the garden until he found Ruth's head pop up in one of the rows. He couldn't see Daisy, but it looked to him like Ruth was trying to help his little sister walk farther in the garden. Ruth's lips were moving, and he longed to know what she was saying.

A sudden wave of anxiety swept over him. It occurred to him that if the two of them were bonding, she might reveal their secret to Daisy, even accidentally. Daisy had kept his secret about wanting to be a musician, but that didn't mean she would hide Ruth's real identity if she knew it.

"Ach, go help her pick the tomatoes. You know you want to. And you better do it quick."

Micah looked at Sadie. "Why is that?"

She nodded toward the barn. "Paul is also watching her. He may go after her first. If he thinks you're dragging your feet about marriage again, I'm certain sure he will make a move on your girl."

Micah followed Paul's gaze and realized that Paul was, indeed, watching Ruth. Micah felt certain that Paul had no interest in Ruth as a bride, but he definitely was up to something.

"Sadie, would you do me a favor?"

"What is it?"

"Would you give Paul some work to do? It appears that his hands may be idle."

Sadie smiled slowly. "I have just the thing." She looked to the outhouse. "He'll be busy for hours. You can count on it." She pushed his shoulder. "Go, chase your dream."

He stared at his sister for a few beats. His dream? If only he could tell her about his *real* dream. In that moment, he saw Paul start to move in Ruth's direction. Micah ran down the porch steps.

"I'll be back by dinner," he called over his shoulder. He ran fast and made it to the garden before Paul. Out of the corner of his eye, Micah saw his brother stop short with a scowl on his face. He'd thwarted Paul's plan, whatever it was, and Paul was none too pleased about it. But Micah didn't care what had been on his little brother's mind. He only wanted to catch up to Ruth and Daisy.

As soon as they came into view, though, he stopped cold.

Ruth was helping Daisy walk without her brace.

"Hey! She's not strong enough to do that." He rushed forward to catch Daisy if she collapsed and hurt herself. But halfway to them, he stopped short when he saw the joy on Daisy's face.

Micah had never seen his sister look so radiant and . . . free.

The look on Micah's face startled Ruth and caused her to reach for Daisy. She scooped the child up in her arms even though she was a little too big to be picked up like that. "I'm sorry if I did something wrong," she said as Micah neared them.

Micah shook his head. He wore an astonished expression. "No, I'm sorry I yelled." He reached out and took his sister from Ruth's arms. "I apologize to you too. I didn't know you could walk like that."

Daisy squirmed in his arms. "I just wanted to try. Don't be mad at Rachel. I wasn't sure I could do it either. I asked her to help me."

Micah met Ruth's gaze over his sister's Kapp. "For a family who is so close, you all sure do keep a lot of secrets from each other," she said. She bit her tongue as she thought she might have insulted him, but his quick smile relieved her concern.

"It's only because we care about each other and don't want to hurt each other," he said. "But I can see why you might think it odd."

Ruth thought of her own sister and how Kathy never held anything back, even if it would hurt Ruth. Maybe even *especially* if it would hurt Ruth. She stared off into the trees above the garden. "Life might have been easier for my sister and me if we had kept some of your kind of secrets." Ruth swallowed hard, not wanting to say more about her family situation, especially in front of Daisy. "Still, it seems hard to be very happy if you have to hide the things that bring you joy." She looked at Daisy, and Daisy gave her a nod of encouragement. "You know you would rather sing than plow fields," she said to Micah.

Daisy smiled and looked up at her brother. "He also likes to *make* music."

"Shh," Micah told his sister while winking at Ruth. "Now you're giving all my secrets away."

"Wait, how exactly do you *make* music?" Ruth smiled. "I'm genuinely interested in hearing this."

"Can we tell her?" Daisy pleaded. "Pleeeeease?"

"I promise I won't tell." Ruth gave Micah a knowing smile. "I think you can trust me."

Micah looked to the sky and pretended to think long and hard. "I suppose you've earned our trust."

Daisy said, "And if you're going to marry her, she has to know!"

Micah sobered at her words, and his smile slipped from his face.

"You don't have to," Ruth said quickly.

"No, no." Micah shook his head, and he seemed to push off the feeling that had come over him. "Daisy's right. If we are to be married, you should know everything."

Ruth caught his smirk before she turned to retrieve Daisy's brace. When she bent down to attach it back into place on the child's leg, Micah knelt at the same time, apparently to do the same thing. Their fingers brushed over the cold metal, sending a strange tingling sensation down Ruth's fingers and up her arm. She let her hand linger for a few breaths while their gazes met.

"I meant what I said," she said quietly. "You don't have to." They both knew they weren't going to be married. He didn't have to share his deepest secrets with her.

She expected him to click the brace in place, but instead, he took it from her hands and put it under his arm.

"How about we let Daisy walk for a little while? I'll hold one hand, and you hold the other. Would you like that?" He looked at his sister.

Daisy's bright smile was the only answer she needed to give.

Micah stood and reached for Daisy's left hand, while Ruth took her right. He pointed them so they could head across the garden, and with slow steps they made their way through the towering tomatoes.

"With both of you helping me, I can move so fast!" Daisy exclaimed. She bestowed a glowing smile on them and then focused with determination back on her steps.

Micah looked at Ruth over the child's head. "This might need to be another secret, Daisy. I don't think Mamm and Daed would be very happy if they saw us."

"Don't worry. I won't tell." Daisy was picking up her steps so high that she practically walked on air between the two of them. She was laughing, and Micah's face reflected the same joy. Once again, Ruth wondered how he would ever say goodbye to these people.

Daisy led the way into the woods and down a path. "It's not much farther now. Right, Micah?"

Micah nodded. "Right past the big tree and along the stream next to that flat rock."

They passed the tree, and the stream came into view. A flat rock about five feet wide stood out. "What's supposed to happen at that rock?" Ruth asked.

"You'll see," Daisy said. "You're in for a treat."

When they reached the rock, Micah lifted Daisy and placed her on it. "This is Daisy's seat."

"It's the perfect rock to sit on," Ruth said. "I assume you both come here often?"

Micah and Daisy shared a knowing smile, and Micah circled around to the other side of the rock. He lifted another rock that was smaller but still looked fairly heavy to Ruth. After he'd set it aside, Micah reached down into the ground and removed a large wooden box with hinges.

"A treasure chest!" Ruth said. "You two are full of secrets." She reached out and tapped Daisy on the nose. The child beamed with excitement.

Micah placed the chest on the flat rock and opened it, and Ruth came around to peek inside. Next, Micah reached in and removed a makeshift guitar with a body made from a cigar box. He placed the instrument on the rock and reached back inside for another. This one appeared to be some kind of a flute made out of a reed. The third instrument he pulled out seemed to be a drum made from a piece of leather stretched over a cross-stitch ring. He passed this one over to Daisy, and the child tapped on the taut material.

Micah held out the flute to Ruth, but she shook her head. "I just want to listen."

He continued to hold it out. "No one's watching. It's only us three."

Ruth glanced around the wooded area. "I suppose you're right." She reached for the flute but wasn't ready to give it a try yet. "I'd still rather hear you."

He sat down and rested the cigar box on his knee, then gave his strings a test with his thumb. The instrument made a sweet noise, but the sound wasn't the best. When Micah started singing along, though, the quality of the guitar didn't matter. Micah's voice was an instrument in itself.

Ruth sat down sideways on the stone and listened while Micah's voice carried on the breeze, singing words of faith and sacrifice for a beloved person. She closed her eyes and took in the sweet melody and lyrics. She had never heard the song before. It occurred to her that the world was missing out by not hearing what she was now hearing. When he finally stopped, silence fell over the woods, an effect that only added to the power of the notes he'd sung.

Ruth whispered, "Did you write that?"

"Ja," he admitted sheepishly. "Do you like it?"

She opened her eyes and looked to see if he was serious. "Like it? I feel so much more than that. It's like it somehow changed me."

"I hope in a *gut* way." His cheeks reddened at her compliment.

Ruth caught the excited sparkle in Daisy's eyes. If only the rest of Micah's family felt the same way about his gift. It wasn't fair that he had to hide this talent. It seemed to her that this went against everything his faith should have taught him.

"Micah, are you sure you've exhausted all measures?" she whispered. She didn't want Daisy to understand everything that his plan would entail. The child believed everything was going to work out perfectly. "Do they know the extent of your talents?"

Micah shook his head. "There's no point." He strummed his fingers over the strings again and closed his eyes. Another song rose to his lips, but this one seemed to spring straight from his saddened heart.

Ruth listened quietly to a song that spoke of how alone the singer felt in a world in which people needed one another. She could tell this was another of Micah's original songs, but when he paused, she wondered if he was also making it up on the spot.

As she watched the strained expression on his face and noted the way his fingers paused before shifting against the strings, she realized that this was indeed the case. Micah's talent knew no bounds. A song that should have brought her to tears suddenly brought her to anger instead.

When he ended the song abruptly, their eyes locked. "I see you finally understand," he said as he took in her expression.

"Ja, I understand," she said. "But that doesn't mean I have to like it." Ruth held her tongue and said no more. She would refrain from saying what she really wanted to say.

For now.

CHAPTER TWELVE

By Monday afternoon, Ruth realized that every moment on the Stolzfus farm had a task assigned to it, and each person had a role in carrying out those tasks. For two hours, Leah had had Ruth grinding cornmeal out of the corn the men had harvested.

The afternoon was hot, and Ruth swiped at her brow as she sat down and watched the ten bags get filled to the brim. "How would you like me to seal these?" she asked when Micah's mother was done.

Ruth could hear the children chattering in their own language and snickering behind her, but Leah shushed them and said, "They're not ready to be sealed yet. We need to add the bay leaves."

Ruth appreciated how patient Leah was with her, even when her children were growing irritated. "Forgive me, but why would you need to put a bay leaf in the cornmeal?"

Sadie spoke up. "To keep away the pests, of course. What does your family use?"

Ruth cringed at the corner she'd backed herself into. "I suppose we just have a spray?"

Leah nodded. "That works too." She gave her children a glare to silence them. "We've just found that it's best to put the leaves right in the bags. We also tape bay leaves to the inside of the pantry door."

Behind Ruth, the children began to whisper. Unbeknownst to them, Connie had been teaching her some Pennsylvania Dutch words over the last few days. She couldn't understand the children completely, but she knew they were speaking negatively. More than anything, Ruth wanted to belong here, but she wasn't sure they felt the same way.

Taking a deep breath, she turned and said in Pennsylvania Dutch, "Danki for teaching me your ways. I haven't done these tasks for as many years as you have, but I am a fast learner." These were the words of reassurance Connie had spoken to her that morning before Micah came to pick her up in the buggy. By turning them on the children, she'd stunned them to silence, and when Ruth looked back at Micah's mother, she was smiling.

Leah walked over to the sacks of cornmeal and began putting the bay leaves inside and sealing them. Ruth joined her, and as they worked, Ruth did something she never did.

She sang out loud for all to hear.

Ruth chose a song Connie had taught her, and soon, everyone was singing along as they worked. She caught the approving gaze from Leah over a sack and smiled. In this moment, everything felt right. Ruth felt like she belonged. There was no spotlight on her, as everyone was contributing. No one was left out. Not even Sadie, who couldn't carry a tune. Though Sadie's notes weren't perfect, her voice still added to the whole song, and the stronger voices smoothed out her broken notes. The scene gave Ruth a better understanding of how the Amish viewed music, and how such moments of order would descend into chaos if Micah became a musician.

But if they could only hear him, she thought.

Even after the song ended, a few of the children continued to hum sweetly. Ruth collected her thoughts and formed the words she had been practicing since she arrived. She could not leave this place before she had at least tried to vouch for Micah.

"Micah would make a wonderful musician."

The humming stopped cold.

Just then the porch door behind them all slapped closed with a resounding smack.

Micah and Paul stood in the doorway. They took in the quiet room with confused looks on their faces.

Ruth wondered how much they'd heard, but her question was immediately answered.

"No Amish woman would ever say such a thing," Paul said.

Micah gave Ruth a questioning look.

"I—we were just singing," she said. "It was a lovely song. I wish you had been here to join in."

Micah shook his head, telling her to stop right now. With a deep sadness, she turned back to the sacks she'd been sealing.

Paul moved closer to Sadie, and she leaned in to whisper in her brother's ear. Ruth figured Sadie was filling him in on what had just transpired. The questioning stare he immediately gave Ruth confirmed her suspicions.

Leah cleared her throat and reached for the first sack of cornmeal. "Rachel, why don't you take the buggy into town and pick up a few things I need for dinner. I'm sure Daisy would love to go with you."

Panic rushed through Ruth. She'd managed to memorize a few lines of a German Amish hymn, but that didn't mean she was ready to handle a horse and buggy. She glanced Micah's way and wondered why he hadn't yet taught her on their morning drive. They had known that this moment would come eventually.

"Actually, Mamm, I need to pick up a few things at the hardware store," Micah said. "I can drive."

Paul said loudly, "I need some things too. Teacher Frannie is getting married in a few weeks, and I need some things for her barn raising."

Leah waved at her sons. "Nonsense. You don't all need to go. Write a list and be efficient."

"I want to go! Thank you, Mamm," Daisy said from where she sat coloring at the table. She quickly returned her crayons to the box and closed her coloring book.

Leah threw up her hands and sighed. "Be back in two hours." She pointed a finger at the boys. "Do not make my dinner late."

Micah reached for Ruth's hand and tugged her toward the door. Paul lifted Daisy from the table and followed them out. The brusque manner with which Micah ushered Ruth out the door told her this wasn't going to be a joyous outing. It was clear that Paul was questioning everything about Ruth. When they all piled into the buggy, Paul placed Daisy in the front seat beside Micah and then settled himself beside Ruth in the back seat. Ruth had no choice but to accept Paul's strange attention.

By the end of the driveway, he was already bombarding her questions. "Tell me about your family. . . ." "What's your favorite meal to cook . . . ?" "Did you ever teach in the schoolhouse?"

Ruth kept her answers concise. Elaborating would only bring on more questions. Many times she caught Micah turning a bit as if he wanted to catch her attention. The horse's hooves clopped loudly against the road, making it impossible for those in the front to overhear the conversation in the back. She could tell by the tight way Micah gripped the reins that he worried about what they were discussing and wanted to put an end to Paul's scrutiny. But they both knew anything he said would only feed Paul's suspicions.

Ruth reminded herself that she had to hold her tongue. The last thing she wanted to do was cause more problems for herself and for Micah. But she could not resist asking one question.

"Look, Paul," she said finally, "your parents sent Micah to Ohio, and Micah brought me home. It seems like that should be enough for you, but obviously it's not. Don't you want your brother to be happy?"

Paul squinted at her. He looked confused by the question. He shrugged again as he tried to formulate an answer.

"I suppose there's nothing wrong with being happy," he said at last. "But who gets to define that happiness? If someone's happiness comes at another's expense, then it's really not from Gött. It's based on pure selfishness. When we work hard, Gött makes us strong through His strength. It's by being committed to community, family, and Gött that we learn how to truly be happy."

Paul stared at the back of his brother's head. Ruth imagined Micah could probably feel his brother's penetrating gaze. She was struck by the realization that all the disdain Paul had shown toward her was, in fact, a function of the heated resentment he actually felt toward his older brother. She had, with her casual question, inadvertently honed in on the source of that disdain.

Micah's attempt to find happiness had, she saw now, resulted in more responsibilities being dropped onto Paul's shoulders. Once again, Ruth questioned the Amish rules that had driven a wedge between the two brothers.

Ruth knew she wouldn't solve the problem between the brothers today. She probably wouldn't solve it at all in her short time in Lititz. But that didn't mean she had to accept it or remain silent about it. From where she sat, it looked like both brothers were in pain.

She weighed her next question carefully. "Let's say that's all true. You carry out your responsibilities completely each day. So if happiness comes from being responsible, then what are you afraid of? What is it about *me* that scares you?"

Paul shifted on the bench, scooting farther from her, and he stayed there throughout the rest of the ride. The atmosphere in the buggy felt tense to Ruth, and by the time Micah had driven the buggy out of the countryside and into a more urban setting, she realized that Paul was unlikely to answer her question. Ruth figured he probably didn't know the answer himself.

Micah pulled the buggy into a parking lot of a strip mall. Ruth saw that a small grocery store and a hardware store were located right next to each other. A few other retail shops stood on the other side of the grocery store. Micah drove the horse over to a wooden shed and pulled the buggy inside. The structure was wide enough for at least three buggies and had a covering for the horse.

Micah stepped down from the buggy and came around the other side to lift Daisy down from the bench. As Ruth stood to follow, Paul remained in his seat. Before she climbed down, he finally spoke.

"Just so you know," he said, "I'm not afraid of you. But I *am* afraid of what will happen when you decide you don't want to be Amish anymore."

Ruth pressed her lips tight as her eyes met Paul's. She had no words that could relieve his fears. Once she left Lititz, he would assume that leaving the Amish was something she had chosen to do. His pointed stare practically dared her to admit that was her plan.

"Rachel," Micah called from below. He tugged on her hand and pulled her attention away from Paul. "We have to keep going."

Ruth turned to look down at him. His words might have well been about their plan—a plan that would tear his family apart—and not just about going into the store.

Paul disembarked from the other side of the buggy and stormed off toward the hardware store with his fists clenched at his sides. Micah's family was already in pain, Ruth realized, and he hadn't even left yet.

"Are you sure about this?" she asked quietly. "About leaving your family? Micah, have you really thought this through?"

Micah glanced at his sister, who was standing at the back of the buggy waiting for them. Under his breath, he said, "I only returned here because of you."

Ruth frowned down at him and gave her hand. Once he'd helped her down, their hands remained clasped. Their faces were less than two inches away from each other. Ruth stared up at him, trying to tell him with her eyes that perhaps the time had come to reconsider his plans.

Micah gave one small shake of his head in answer. Ruth realized that whether or not she agreed to help, Micah was not long for the Amish life.

And Paul knew it.

CHAPTER THIRTEEN

As Ruth and Daisy approached the automatic door of the grocery store, Ruth caught sight of her reflection in the glass and realized her Kapp had slipped back on her head. She righted the fabric and pressed her dress flat just as two Amish women exited the store, pushing a small cart of groceries. The double takes they gave Ruth conveyed their surprise at seeing an Amish woman they didn't recognize.

They stopped, and the older of the women spoke to Daisy in Pennsylvania Dutch.

"This is Rachel Miller. She might marry Micah. She speaks English, though," Daisy responded, also in Pennsylvania Dutch.

Both women raised their eyebrows.

"Is that so?" The woman changed to English. "Well, either way, welcome to Lititz and to the community. I'm Emily Bontrager, and this is my daughter Deborah."

The younger of the two women appeared to be about five years older than Ruth. She seemed less worried by Ruth's presence. "I do hope we'll see your engagement announcement in the paper soon. The holidays are almost here, and wedding season will be over for another year. So don't diddle-daddle." She smiled, exposing a set of dimples in her cherublike face.

"I do hope our paths will cross again," Ruth said.

When they smiled warmly, she knew her words were acceptable, and she hadn't broken any rules. She relaxed enough to return their warm grins and said, "Do you live close to the Stolzfus family?"

"Ja, Mamm and I live about a mile down the road. Just past the farm with three silos. You know, the red ones," the cheery woman responded. "I do hope you'll visit, Rachel."

Ruth struggled to keep a frown from her face. For a moment, she had felt heartened by the possibility of a blossoming friendship. But Deborah thought she was Rachel, and Ruth knew that no friendship would ever grow out of a lie. Micah's own family was falling apart because they were ignoring an important truth. What she was doing was no different.

Ruth told herself that it was just as well that she and Deborah couldn't become friends, since she would not be here for very long. But that didn't make the loss hurt any less.

"It was nice to meet you as well," she said with a forced smile. "I look forward to getting to know you."

Her words sounded good anyway.

The older woman pursed her lips. "I can't place your accent. Where did you say you are from?"

Daisy chimed in. "She's from the Northwest. We all make fun of the way she talks too."

The three adults laughed, albeit a little uneasily. The older woman said, "We should be getting along." She looked down at Daisy. "Don't be late for your Mamm's dinner."

Daisy shook her head. "We won't. We have a list." She held up a slip of paper her mother had given them. And with that, Ruth and Daisy headed into the store. If the women suspected that Ruth wasn't telling the truth, they didn't let on.

Ruth and Daisy walked down the condiment aisle, where four Englisch boys around eleven or twelve years of age were shouting something. Ruth was focused on finding a particular spice that Leah wanted, and she didn't pay the boys any mind.

A moment later, she heard a loud crash. Both she and Daisy jumped at the sound. The boys at the end of the aisle had dropped a jar of pickles, smashing it to pieces. A look of horror came over a few of them, and they ran past Ruth and disappeared at the end of the aisle. Two others stayed behind, laughing.

"Rachel, I'm scared," Daisy said in a harsh whisper.

One of the boys must've heard her because he laughed even louder. As he drew closer, he began to limp in an exaggerated manner.

The crestfallen look on Daisy's face twisted Ruth's stomach into a knot. She remembered feeling like an outcast after her parents died. The stares of other teenagers had only made her feel worse at a time when it was all she could do to just put one foot in front of the other. Ruth had learned to cope by flying under the radar. By not bringing attention to herself.

Daisy didn't have that option.

If the children had been making fun of Ruth, she would have just walked away and kept to herself. But walking away wouldn't help Daisy now. No child should have to fear going to the grocery store. It occurred to Ruth that perhaps she wouldn't have been so isolated as a teen if she had been able to help other kids face their fear of not knowing what to say to her. Even if she hadn't succeeded, she would have walked away holding her head high.

And now, so could Daisy.

Ruth turned to the boy, who was about to pass them. She dug down deep and, drawing as much strength as she could muster, said, "You know, she's just like you and only wants to be accepted."

The boy stumbled a bit, but he caught himself and quickly began walking correctly. He dropped his head down as he passed by. It wasn't exactly the response Ruth had hoped for, but speaking out for Daisy felt right. She actually felt exhilarated and empowered.

She stood up straighter and called after the boy, "You can make this right and fix this right now. I promise you that you'll feel better."

The boy stopped and flipped his brown hair out of his eyes as he turned back toward them. He glanced at the end of the aisle, but his friend was gone now. The boy turned back to Ruth and Daisy, and the look he gave them betrayed the distaste he clearly felt, but Ruth offered him a sweet smile that she hoped would defuse any embarrassment or anger that was rising in him. He dropped his gaze to the floor.

"I'm sorry," he mumbled, giving Ruth a fleeting glance.

With her smile still in place, Ruth said, "That's nice, but how about you say it to her?"

The boy lifted his head and looked at Daisy. "Sorry about your leg, and I'm sorry I made fun of you." The boy looked back at Ruth as if to ask whether that was good enough.

Ruth continued to smile. "What's your name?"

The boy hesitated and then mumbled, "Tom."

"I'm Rachel, and this is Daisy. It's very nice to meet you, Tom."

The wideness of the boy's eyes told her that he had probably never spoken to any of the Amish people in his community before. She hoped he would see that they were people just like him.

Except, she really wasn't Amish, so perhaps she wasn't the best person to be building this particular bridge. Still, it felt good to speak up. Maybe if she had spoken up about Taylor Williams in the first place, she wouldn't have wound up homeless and jobless, in Lititz, pretending to be someone she wasn't.

But then she wouldn't have been here to help Daisy.

Or this boy.

Ruth looked down at the smashed jar of pickles in the aisle. "You should probably find someone to help you clean that up too."

The boy gave a half-hearted nod and headed down the aisle. As he reached the end of it, Ruth noticed a blond Amish woman standing there, watching their interaction.

Daisy's face lit up as she noticed the woman too. "Teacher Frannie!" Daisy stepped slowly toward the young woman, and Ruth followed. The teacher appeared to be about two years younger than Ruth, which would make her about nineteen. She didn't seem old enough to Ruth to be a teacher, but Ruth didn't really know what credentials the Amish required in the classroom. She wondered if this was the teacher Paul had mentioned was getting married. She seemed so young, but then Ruth also knew that at age twenty-four, Micah was already way past the age when he was expected to have married. The Amish community probably looked at Ruth and thought she was far too old to be single.

"I'm Rachel," Ruth introduced herself. She tried not to cringe as she said the words.

"And I'm impressed." The young teacher smiled. She put out her hand to shake Ruth's. "I'm Frannie, the schoolteacher. Pardon my boldness, but is there any way you might consider helping out at the school? The way you handled that situation was perfect. I have a wedding to plan, and I could really use help in the classroom for a few weeks."

The look Daisy gave Ruth was one of pure joy. "Oh, Rachel, you have to!"

Ruth sputtered a few syllables while her mind processed what Frannie had just said. "Y-you want me to help you teach? You don't even know me."

The teacher touched her arm. "If the Stolzfus family approved of you, then I approve of you. Plus, I just saw you work wonders

with that boy." She glanced around and then back at Ruth with a
frown. "Between you and me, I have another student in my school
who is heading in the same direction."

"I have to be honest with you. I'm not trained to help in a
classroom."

"It's only for a few weeks. The new teacher will take over after
my wedding."

Ruth looked at her in confusion. "You won't teach after you
marry?"

Frannie's eyebrows furrowed, and Ruth realized she'd chosen
her words unwisely again. She wondered what she'd said wrong
this time.

"You must have some different Ordnung where you come
from." Frannie laughed nervously. "Our schoolteachers only work
until we marry. Then we leave to make our homes as Fraa."

"Right. Of course." Ruth tried to think of an explanation, but
none came to mind, so she said nothing more about it. "I'd like to
consider your offer tonight. Would you mind?"

"Nee, not at all. Come to the school tomorrow with Daisy and
her siblings. Spend the day with us before deciding. I'm certain
sure you will enjoy it." Frannie winked at Daisy. "Ja?"

Daisy nodded emphatically. "It will be grand!" She took hold
of Ruth's hand. "It will make me so happy to have you with me all
day."

Ruth smiled down at the child. Daisy's care for her warmed
her heart, but she worried that Daisy was becoming so attached to
her. If for no other reason than to keep Daisy from becoming even
more connected to her, Ruth should decline the offer. But a stirring of excitement within her kept her from saying no on the spot.

"I would love to join your class tomorrow. Thank you." Ruth
meant every word. Telling the truth was so much easier than telling lies.

Once Frannie left them, Ruth and Daisy finished up their shopping and exited the store into the late afternoon fall sun. Ruth shielded her eyes against the glare, but as she turned her face to the side, the sunlight captured an object in the window of the store next door.

There in the front display was a small mandolin. Its smooth, dark brown finish glinted in the light.

"Oh, Daisy, would you mind if we go into the music store?"

Daisy's eyes widened. She appeared nervous but also excited. She looked in the window and drew in a breath. "Ach, Micah would love that."

Ruth nodded. "That's what I was thinking too. Come on, let's go see how much it is."

"But, Rachel, instruments aren't allowed."

"I know," Ruth said. "So it will need to be a secret. Just like his other instruments that he made. Micah will need something real if he's going to perform."

Daisy nodded. "That's true." She looked around at the near-empty parking lot. "Hurry! Let's go in before someone sees us."

Ruth took Daisy's elbow and guided the child next door as quick as she could possibly go. At the entrance, she glanced back to be sure they hadn't been spotted. The coast was clear, and less than ten minutes later, they walked out of the store with the instrument in hand. The store owner put it in a protective cloth covering, but anyone could tell by its shape that it was an instrument.

"Let's hide it in the back of the buggy," Daisy said as she untied her apron. "Use my apron to cover it up so Paul and Micah don't see it. It will be a surprise for later."

The child was giddy with excitement. Ruth helped her into the buggy's back seat and sat beside her. When the men returned, Ruth clenched her fists on her legs and struggled to remain calm.

Micah and Paul settled onto the front bench and looked back at them. "Is everything all right?" Paul asked as he took up the reins. "You two look like you're up to something."

Ruth shook her head. "Not at all. But we better get going before Mamm scolds us for being late."

Micah's smirk fell from his lips as he locked his gaze on her. He appeared concerned by what she'd said for some reason, and maybe even a little sad. But she felt too excited to worry about whatever she'd said wrong this time. All that mattered was giving him his gift. Ruth knew the mandolin would make Micah happy again. She couldn't wait to see his face when she handed him the gift of music.

The gift of his own heart.

CHAPTER FOURTEEN

Micah sat in the passenger seat while his brother drove them home. In his mind, he could still hear Ruth calling his mother *Mamm* as naturally as if she had been doing it her whole life. How quickly she had fit into his family. Why hadn't he thought this whole thing through? With each passing day, she was becoming more and more invested in life here. The whole ride home, he sat in silence, wondering if she would be able to really leave when the time came for her to go.

Paul pulled into the barn and locked the buggy into place. "Can you put the horse away?"

Micah nodded. "Please take Daisy inside with you," he said under his breath.

Paul glanced his way and whispered, "I hope this glum look on your face means you've come to your senses."

"Ja, I have." Micah knew there was only one thing he could do. He had to think of Ruth and forget about his plan. Hurting her hadn't been part of the bargain. He had to let her go before she got any more attached to his family.

"Gut." Paul stepped down, and then he lifted Daisy from her seat and carried her out the barn doors.

"What's the matter?" Ruth asked from the seat behind Micah. "You've been awfully quiet the whole ride home. Did I say something wrong?"

Micah stepped down from the buggy and gazed up at her. "You have done amazing things here. You have upheld your end of the bargain and then some." He shook his head. "But I never realized what I was asking of you."

Ruth waved a hand at him. "I haven't done anything that I didn't want to. Your family is a joy, and I am learning so much."

Micah sighed. "That's what I was afraid of."

Ruth studied him. "I feel like I've disappointed you in some way. I'm not sure how. But there's one thing that might help. I bought you a present. May I give it to you now?"

"A present?" Micah swallowed hard. "Ruth, this is what I'm saying. You just give and give, and I can't reciprocate."

Ruth stood and held out her hand for him to help her down from the buggy. He did, and she hopped down right in front of him. When she looked up at him, her eyes sparkled with excitement. He needed to send her away, but she obviously didn't understand what he was trying to do. She wouldn't be smiling if she did.

"You give me just as much." She reached up and touched his cheek, tapping it gently. "My life changed so much the moment I met you, Micah Stolzfus." Her hand dropped to his chest, then she tapped him there too. "I'll be right back." She disappeared around the back of the buggy.

Micah's mind whirled. He couldn't believe the way he was messing this up. He really *did* ruin everything, just like Paul said. "Ruth," he said in her direction. "I think I need to bring you—"

Just then, Ruth stepped out from behind the rear of the buggy, holding a mandolin. The words Micah had been about to speak froze in his mouth. He didn't know which was more beautiful: the brand-new instrument or the woman holding it.

"Is that for me?" He forced the words from his mouth. He looked at her, dumbfounded.

She brought it to him and placed it in his hands. "Try it."

"Ruth, I shouldn't have this," he said, but his eyes were devouring the mandolin. "It's so beautiful. I've never held a real instrument in my life." The temptation to play overcame him, and he brought it to his chest to strum. The melodious sound it made calmed his racing heart.

"It sounds wonderful," she whispered. "Can you play a song? Can you play the one you wrote?" She led him over to some hay bales and sat down, making room for him to sit beside her. She patted the spot, and he followed her instruction, as if he were in a trance. He didn't know how close anyone else might be, so he played the instrument lightly and matched his voice to the low sound so that only he and Ruth could hear.

Ruth closed her eyes as he sang to her. Her eyelashes fluttered against her creamy white cheeks. There was a touch of natural blush along her cheekbones, brought on by her exuberance. This gift had come from her heart. The stunning woman in front of him took his breath away. Her soft lips and a slight smile made him want to draw close to her. Without realizing it, Micah leaned in while he sang softly.

Her eyelashes lifted slowly, and she drew in a sharp breath. Micah expected her to either pull away or push him away.

She did neither.

He strummed softly as his song came to an end. The last note reverberated between them until the only sound left was the sound of them breathing.

She whispered, "Do you like it?"

Micah nodded as he looked at her lips. He pressed his own lips together and told himself not to lean forward any more than he already had. He swallowed hard. "It's the best present I've ever received. I can't think of anything I could want more, except . . ."

She dropped her gaze to his lips. "I think I understand. You can kiss me, if you want." She tipped her head up toward his, and he leaned forward to capture her lips.

Sure, he had thought about kissing Ruth, but never could he have imagined what it would be like, nor the effect her lips would actually have on him. In that moment, it was as if everything he had previously deemed important slipped away forever.

The mandolin in his hands slipped away too, and with his eyes still closed and his lips still on Ruth's, he placed the instrument gently on the hay beside him. Now that his hands were free, he reached up to touch her cheeks, and he deepened the kiss, losing himself in it completely.

"This is not what I had in mind when I asked you if you had come to your senses." Paul's voice startled Micah back to reality.

Separating himself from Ruth was the hardest thing he'd ever had to do. But they both pulled away, and Ruth rose to her feet. He watched her wobble a bit, and she reached out to the buggy to steady herself. She covered her mouth with her free hand and stared at Paul in horror.

Only Micah noticed that Paul wasn't looking at Ruth. He was looking at something on the hay bale.

Micah glanced to his side and saw the mandolin on the hay. He looked back at Paul. Micah had never seen his brother's face so red with anger.

"I can explain." Micah reached for the instrument. He really had no idea what he planned to say. He had no excuse that the Amish would accept, and his mind was still whirling from the kiss he'd shared with Ruth. All he wanted to do was kiss her again.

"There is nothing you can say to make any of this right," Paul said in a tight voice. "You have disgraced our family and the community." He turned and stomped out of the barn.

"I'm so sorry," Ruth said into the ensuing silence. "I only wanted to bring you joy."

Micah held his tongue to keep from speaking what was in his heart. The truth was that Ruth already brought him joy just by being herself.

She headed toward the doors but stopped at the back of the buggy. "I decided to help at the schoolhouse during the day," she said. "Perhaps I won't complicate your relationships anymore if I'm not here as much. I'll also start looking for a place to live. I'm so sorry that I've made things worse for you and your family."

She turned then and rushed out the doors. Micah wanted to stop her, but words would not form on his lips. He was also certain sure that if he went after her, he would only kiss her again.

Dinner with Micah's family had been nearly impossible to get through. Ruth had said barely two words, and Paul hadn't said even one. The heated glare he aimed at Micah had been impossible for the others to miss. Ruth and Micah's buggy ride back to Aunt Connie's little house had been just as tense as dinner, as Paul had jumped into the passenger seat to join them. All he'd said to them was that they needed a chaperone. But Ruth didn't know what had made him more upset—the fact that she'd bought Micah an instrument or that he'd caught them kissing.

She was still in a bit of shock over that development herself.

Ruth ran inside and closed the door to Connie's home behind her. As soon as it was shut, she leaned back against the cool wood. She closed her eyes and took a couple of deep breaths.

"Sounds like tonight may have been a bit too much to handle," Connie said from her rocking chair. Her knitting needles clacked along with her words. "My sister's family can be a lot all at once.

That's why I moved out here. And that was *before* she had eight children." Connie laughed softly.

Ruth had yet to open her eyes. She just wasn't ready. She lifted her hand and touched her lips. They still felt a little puffy from Micah's kiss. She'd only kissed one other person in her life, and Taylor Williams had been a terrible disappointment. But then, what could she expect from someone who had only been using her? He had kissed her, but not because he truly wanted to. Micah, on the other hand . . . ?

Ja, he wanted to.

And if Paul hadn't walked in . . . Well, she thought, they just might still be kissing.

"Is everything all right, dear?" Connie asked. The sound of her knitting needles stopped, and her feet could be heard shuffling.

"Nee, nothing's all right. I'm afraid I've made a big mistake."

"In what way?" Connie stood in the doorway to the front room.

"I make a horrible Amish woman. Paul hates me and—"

"Paul? Why on earth would Paul hate you? And why does it matter? You're not marrying Paul."

Ruth opened her eyes and stared at the ceiling. "Oh, Connie, tonight was horrible. He's always trying to catch me making wrong choices. He did it all day today, and then, right before dinner, he caught us . . ." Ruth cleared her throat. "Well, you know."

Connie was quiet for a few moments, and then a little giggle erupted from her lips. Ruth looked her way and found the woman smiling.

"What's so funny?" Ruth was growing more confused by the Amish every day.

"He caught you *bossing*?"

Ruth didn't know what that meant. She didn't want to say yes in case it went beyond kissing. *That* would be a million times worse. Ruth supposed kissing wasn't too catastrophic.

"Isn't kissing expected when you're courting?" Ruth asked, hoping she wasn't saying something wrong again.

"Absolutely. And a lot of it." Connie's smile widened. "So, how was it?"

"Aunt Connie! I don't think I should talk about such things." Ruth made her way to the sofa, and Connie joined her. As she fell back on the seat cushions, she thought about how Micah had held her face in his palms and kissed her so thoroughly. Her toes curled again just remembering the feel of his urgent lips against her own. "I feel like I've found something I'd thought was lost forever."

Connie sighed. "Ach, I love that. What a beautiful sentiment to think on. The two of you will be so happy."

Ruth squeezed her eyes shut. She wanted to be honest with this woman for once. But how could she admit to having lied to everyone? "Connie, what if I'm not what makes Micah happy? What if there's something else that his heart longs for even more?"

Connie waved a hand her way. "Don't be ridiculous. He's crazy about you."

Ruth studied Connie's face. The woman beamed with a giddiness Ruth hadn't seen her show before. It dawned on her that Connie might be reliving the days of her own schooltime love.

"What was his name?" Ruth asked carefully. "The young man you . . . cared about?"

Connie's smile flickered, but it didn't fade away. "Josiah," she whispered, almost reverently. Then she cupped her hand as if making a little megaphone out of it and whispered, "He was a good kisser too."

"Connie! I'm shocked." Ruth giggled.

Connie waggled a finger at her. "I'll deny it if you tell anyone."

"Not to worry. My lips are sealed." The clock ticked on the wall over the fireplace. "Would you tell me about him?" Ruth asked. "I mean, if you're comfortable doing so."

Connie faced Ruth. Even though Connie could not see her, Ruth knew that she was seeing something. The glow of old memories softened her face.

"I won't go into all the details, as those are mine and I hold them close to me. But I will say that I still wonder what might have come of us if his family hadn't gotten involved. Would we live here, or would I have joined him in his community? Would I be as self-reliant as I am? Or would we really have ended up as dependent on his family as they feared we would?"

"So, his family convinced him to marry a seeing person?"

Connie nodded, and for the first time, her eyes glistened with unshed tears. "I still remember the day my Mamm read me the wedding announcement in *The Budget*. Up until then, I had hoped he would still come for me."

Ruth took Connie's hand in hers. "I'm so sorry. Families do not always know what's best. They should have let the two of you decide for yourselves."

Connie shrugged. "Ach, who knows? Maybe they were right. If something horrible had happened to Josiah, I would not have been able to help him."

"You don't sound like you believe that."

"It doesn't matter what I believe. It never did. I cherish the time Josiah and I shared together at school, back when it was just the two of us making crazy plans we both knew would never come to pass. At some point, I suppose, reality had to take over."

Her words twisted Ruth's insides. Reality was something both she and Micah had been avoiding. She needed to find a place to live, and he needed to find his place in his community. The truth was, she wasn't helping in the way she'd hoped to. Micah expected her to help him leave, but that no longer felt like a good idea to Ruth. And although Micah was the most talented musician she'd ever heard, she knew that he wasn't prepared to live in the Englisch world. Nor was he truly prepared to live a life without his family.

"Plans are fun, though," Ruth said. "But you're right. Reality will rear its head. Thank you for sharing with me. You've helped me so much with settling into the Stolzfus family. And tomorrow, I'll start helping Teacher Frannie at the school."

"Rachel, that's wonderful! You will bless those children so much with your warmth and joy. Do you know how to get to the schoolhouse?"

"Ja, I pass by it on the way to Micah's. I plan to walk each day. It will be *gut* exercise."

"For certain sure."

There was also a convenience store on the way, and Ruth planned to stop there and buy a newspaper. She needed to snap back into reality and find an apartment. Once that decision was made, she found herself wondering if there was any way to help Micah have the best of both worlds.

"Connie, can you tell me why the only music allowed is hymns and work songs?"

Connie tilted her head at Ruth. "I don't understand what you mean?"

"I was just thinking about Micah and how wonderful his voice is. You must realize that, don't you?"

Connie leaned forward with a serious expression on her face. Ruth prepared herself for a scolding. After all, Paul had made it clear that no Amish woman would ever say the words she'd just spoken.

"Rachel, I care about you, so I am telling you this out of love. I can only assume Micah has shared his dream of being a musician with you, ja?"

So Connie *did* know. Micah's secret was not a secret at all. It was just a fact that everyone ignored. Ruth hated knowing this. Part of her had hoped that the family might embrace Micah's talent and encourage it, if only they knew about it.

"He has told me, and I only want to see him happy."

"Even if that means he has to leave the Amish?"

"Nee," Ruth said quietly. "I know he won't be happy with the Englisch. He needs his family. But why can't he have both music *and* family?"

Connie reached out her hand to Ruth's face. Ruth let the woman's gentle touch comfort her. "For the same reason I could not have my Josiah. Fighting for what I wanted would have only brought strife and chaos to the community. We strive for peace, no matter the personal cost."

"But why would his singing not be peaceful? You should have heard him today. I tend to be anxious, but the song he wrote relieved me of that feeling. It brought me peace. It was all about faith and sacrifice . . ." Her voice trailed off.

Suddenly, Micah's song made sense. Deep down, even he knew his musical career would never happen.

"Then that is a gift the two of you will share in your future home."

The truth clung to Ruth's tongue. How she wanted to tell Connie that she would never share a home with Micah. "I don't think it will be enough for him. He thinks he wants . . . more."

Connie sighed. "That's been a worry that my sister has had for quite some time."

Ruth thought of the bride-to-be whom Micah was actually intended to have returned with. The real Rachel would have walked into this situation having no idea why she'd really been chosen. A family was what was really at stake. One man's happiness would come at a great cost to many.

"Honestly," Ruth said, "when I was younger, something horrible happened to my family. It really broke us apart. I know what it feels like to lose the people closest to me. I don't want that for the Stolzfus family. I don't want that for Micah." The words she spoke were all true.

But leaving his family is exactly what I agreed to help him do.

Connie leaned closer and pulled Ruth into a comforting embrace. "Ach, child, I am so sorry to hear this. I never asked about the home you came from, but perhaps I should have, especially knowing that your family arranged your wedding, just as Micah's did. A person can justify nearly any action. Micah's parents certainly had their reasons for doing what they did."

Ruth thought about the real Rachel, who had rejected Micah immediately. She surely had a reason for doing so, one that most likely had nothing to do with Micah. Did her heart yearn for someone her family was keeping her from?

"Do you think Gött has brought me here for a reason? I've never put much thought into Him being involved in our lives," Ruth admitted. "I've never really felt Him working in mine." She let the statement end there. She'd always thought if there was a Gött, He must have overlooked her.

"Gött loves us and always wants what's best for us. So, ja, I would say you have been brought to the Stolzfus family to make sure they remain intact. I believe in my heart that you, dear Rachel, are the missing piece this family has needed. I know how music is important to Micah. But I also know that you are just as important to him. Even more so."

"I don't know about that. You should see him sing when no one is around." Ruth cringed at her choice of words. "I mean, not see him, but—"

Connie pulled back and stared into Ruth's face. "I know what you mean. I may be blind, but I have seen how music transforms him. But, sweet Rachel, I've also seen how *you* have transformed him."

Ruth sighed, wishing she could tell Connie the real reason for Micah's transformation. As far as he was concerned, she wasn't the missing piece that would keep his family together. She was his one-way ticket out.

Ruth knew she was not living up to the bargain she and Micah had struck. She no longer wanted to help him escape his life. What she wanted more than anything was to find a way for him to be a musician and keep his family intact too.

She also knew that if she reneged on their deal, he just might hate her forever.

CHAPTER FIFTEEN

Dark clouds loomed above as the morning unfolded at the Stolzfus farm. Micah had already been out in the fields for an hour when rain began to mist down on him from the sky. The corn that would be used for the animals' feed through the winter still needed to be picked, so the harvest was not yet complete. The farmer's life held few reprieves. Another reason why he looked forward to a life on the road. He just didn't have it in him to do this for the rest of his life.

Paul was making his way across the field with sure and fast steps. Micah braced himself to hear whatever was on his brother's mind. Paul's mission to discredit Ruth was wearing thin. Micah hadn't expected his brother to take on this crusade against her. In fact, Paul was the one person Micah had expected to embrace her, since once Micah was settled, Paul would be free to find a girl of his own. Micah had always told his brother not to wait for him, but Paul tended to obey their father even in the small things, and he skewed toward old-fashioned ways.

"Whoa." Micah pulled back on his horse's reins. He brought the horse-powered tractor to a stop and locked it as Paul drew close. "You come out here to help?"

"I've done plenty. I'd say it's about time you do your part." Paul lifted his chin in defiance. "There's a reason we follow a set of rules. Do what you're supposed to do, and things go smoothly for all." He removed a piece of paper from his pocket. "I made a phone call."

Micah warily watched him unfold the piece of paper. "We don't own a phone. How is that following the rules?"

"It's approved when it's necessary. And Elder Joseph approved it." Paul raised his eyebrows at Micah as if waiting for him to come clean about something.

"What have you done, Paul?"

"What I should have done the first day she arrived. You'll never guess who I talked to on the phone."

Micah had an idea, but he kept his lips sealed.

Paul shook his head at Micah. "Last night after dinner, I tried to figure out why she would give you a mandolin. It made no sense. Even if she doesn't come from an old order, musical instruments are never allowed. It doesn't matter what community someone is from. I decided to call Rachel's parents and ask them if there was something we should know about her."

Micah felt a chill fall over him. "Anything you wanted to know about her you could have found out by asking her. Just like you have been doing. Or you could have asked me."

"Y-you?" Paul sputtered. "You can't be honest about anything!"

"Calm down."

"This *is* calm. You should have seen me last night. I nearly woke you up when I got in, but I was so mad, I thought better of it. I decided to sleep on it. I hoped maybe I wouldn't throttle you if I waited until the morning."

"So what now? Are you going to do it?" Micah bit his tongue. He knew better than to encourage such behavior. The Amish don't fight.

Paul flapped the paper at Micah. "That depends. Are you going to come clean about who that woman is? Because we both know she is not Rachel Miller. The real Rachel Miller is still in Ohio. I know this because I talked to her. So, who is this imposter? And give me one good reason why I shouldn't go tell Daed this very minute."

Micah's heart fell. So, the secret was out.

He'd never thought his brother would be the one to take his plan down. Micah looked at the house and saw his Mamm driving the kids to school. Daisy sat up front and waved exuberantly as the buggy went down the driveway.

"I'll give you two reasons. Mamm and Daisy. They both adore Rachel and would be crushed by this news. You heard how happy they were when they learned that Rachel would be helping Teacher Frannie for a few weeks."

"But she's not *Rachel*." Paul's jaw ticked.

"She's the woman in my life," Micah said evenly, "and that's all that matters. Daed just wanted me to get married. It wasn't like he had met the girl he chose for me. It could have been anyone."

Paul squinted. "So you went out and found someone on your own instead? You had years to do this. Why now?"

Micah shrugged. "I went and met the Rachel of Ohio. She wasn't interested."

"She did tell me that," Paul said smugly. It was clear that he enjoyed throwing that fact in Micah's face.

"What do you suppose Daed would have done if I returned home without her? What do you suppose he would have thought?"

Paul looked to the hills behind Micah. Some of his smugness drained away. His anger also appeared to thaw a bit. "Ach, he probably would have traveled back to get her himself."

"Exactly. He wouldn't have believed that I wasn't the one who broke off the arrangement. He would have thought I was only putting off getting married again. I had to do something. Rachel, *my* Rachel, offered to help. To fill in for the other one."

"You expect me to believe her name is Rachel too?"

"It doesn't matter if it is. And it doesn't matter what you believe."

"Fine, but I'm still telling."

Micah shook his head. "You can't. Rachel and I have a plan. We're working it out. In a couple weeks, everything will be made right. You'll see. And I promise you, you'll be happy."

"Why would I be happy?"

"Because, Bruder," Micah said, "you will finally have everything you ever wanted."

The Amish schoolhouse was nothing like what Ruth had expected. Bright yellow walls, modern school desks, and plastic chairs greeted her, and brightly colored children's artwork hung on the walls. There was a woodstove at the front of the classroom that, come winter, would keep the schoolroom toasty.

Teacher Frannie welcomed her in with a warm embrace. It was clear that she was genuinely happy to have Ruth there. "I'm sure it's not that different from the schoolhouse you attended," she said as Ruth stood at the front of the classroom, taking it all in.

Ruth wasn't up to maintaining a lie of this scale. She wouldn't be able to fake an understanding of the Amish learning style. "Actually, I attended a public school when I was little. My family wasn't always Amish, and when we converted, I stayed at my school because I needed special education for some learning disabilities." This last part was true. She had always struggled with being put on the spot. Her anxiety would always shut down her brain, rendering her unable to learn anything.

"Ja? I've heard some Amish will put their children in Englisch school for specific reasons. I just have never met anyone who had been to the other side." Teacher Frannie's smile and twinkling eyes told Ruth she was in a safe place. She felt no judgment from Frannie, and the woman's sweetness seemed real. Ruth found herself hoping they would become great friends. Then she remembered she would be gone in a couple of weeks.

The newspaper in her satchel reminded her of that . . . and saddened her.

Regardless, Ruth needed to focus on finding an apartment. But first, she needed to learn how she'd be spending her days until it was time for her to leave. "Can you show me around and explain what you need from me?"

"For certain sure. The children will be arriving soon. Most of them walk to school, but some families who live far out on the outskirts of the community will drive them in." Frannie then explained what she used each individual chalkboard for. She said that she would especially need Ruth to help the kids with their math. Then Frannie's face paled. "Ach, I didn't even think that maybe you . . . I mean, if you had learning disabilities, that maybe you—"

Ruth realized what she was trying to say in a diplomatic way. "Math has always been my strong suit. Give me numbers any day. I'm more concerned about standing up in front of the class and having to speak. That's where I might fail you."

"You will not fail me at all." Frannie tapped her finger on her chin as though she was thinking about something. "In fact, I believe the children will love that you are able to help them do their figuring quietly and independently, without the whole class watching them. You'll probably reach them better than I can at the head of the room. And the fact that you're stronger in English than in Pennsylvania Dutch will give them language practice." Frannie smiled. "Ja, this is going to be perfect." She looked at the clock just as the sound of children laughing and shrieking began to filter in through the open windows. "It's time. They'll play outside until I ring them in. But do you have any questions?"

"A ton?" Ruth wouldn't lie about her doubts either. "But I think I'll spread them out throughout the day."

Frannie laughed. "Feel free to interrupt me anytime you need to. But I know you will do fine."

"Rachel?" A sweet, familiar voice could be heard at the window. Ruth looked up and saw Daisy peering inside.

"Ja, Daisy, I am here," Ruth said.

"Yay! Rachel's going to be helping me!" Daisy shouted to someone out in the yard.

Frannie headed to the door to round up the children. "See? The children are already excited to have you here. Enjoy the day, Rachel. It's going to be tiring, but in a *gut* way. I'm sure you will find it rewarding."

Ruth stayed back as the teacher headed out. As she circled the room, Ruth wondered what on earth she had been thinking when she took on this role. She felt her chest constrict and her breath grow short. She placed a hand on her stomach in an attempt to settle her nerves. Frannie had promised that she wouldn't have to speak from the front of the classroom. There would be no spotlights on her, only the eyes of the children.

Ruth turned back toward the door and saw at least twenty pairs of eyes staring at her. The children gawked in silence.

"Guder Daag, children," Ruth spoke. "I'm Rachel, and I like math. Does that make me strange?"

The children erupted in giggles and raced to their seats as Frannie came back into the room. One little boy stopped and pulled on Ruth's dress. He cupped his hand, and Ruth bent down to hear what he had to say.

"I like math too," he whispered.

Ruth whispered back, "What's your name?"

"Simon." He raced to his seat at the front of the class, and Frannie winked in Ruth's direction. Ruth felt a warm confidence rise in her chest and spread throughout her body. She smiled.

She had won the children over, and she had done it just by being herself.

CHAPTER SIXTEEN

Micah sang a new song he was working on as he drove the horse and buggy up to the schoolhouse. He was a few minutes early, and the children hadn't emerged with their usual shouts of joy at being released from lessons. Beside him on the seat was a wicker picnic basket filled with an afternoon snack of warm apple strudel that Sadie and Mamm had made. Mamm had put some in the basket and asked him to pick up Daisy. But when she told him to have the other siblings walk home, he knew she was hinting for him to pick up Ruth as well. He lifted the lid and smirked. The extra portion of strudel and the blanket inside confirmed his suspicions.

Could his mother be any more obvious?

Not that Micah minded—especially since he needed to speak to Ruth about Paul. He dropped the lid closed and tried to think of the best place for their picnic snack.

The first location that came to mind was the stream behind the old Zook farm . . . or, more accurately, his farm now. Micah still found it difficult to think of the land as his, especially since he knew he never planned to farm it. Daed had purchased it last year as a way to push Micah into finding a Fraa. When that didn't work, Daed had found the bride too.

So why bring Ruth to the place? What would be the point? It wasn't as though the place would ever hold any significant meaning for them.

And yet, as he watched Ruth come his way, he knew that was where he would take her.

"Mamm has a treat for you all at home," Micah said to his siblings. "You all will get there faster than the buggy. Especially since I'll be stopping off at Aunt Connie's to drop Rachel off."

His brothers and sisters raced toward home as he lifted Daisy into the back seat. Then he turned and offered Ruth his hand to help her up.

"I can walk," she said, not taking his hand. "It's not far at all."

"Nee, we need to talk." He let her know with his solemn face that something was amiss.

She nodded and took his hand and then settled into the front bench. Soon the reins were in Micah's hands, and he had the buggy in motion. But he didn't take the turnoff for Aunt Connie's.

"Where are we going?" Daisy asked. Ruth gave him a look that said she was wondering the same thing.

"You'll see," Micah said and was glad they left it at that. Twenty minutes later, he pulled into the driveway of the old Zook farm. Thomas Zook had died without children, and he had left his property to the community. Elder Joseph had arranged for Daed to purchase the land for a fair price. The property also had a house and several outbuildings.

"Whose house is this?" Ruth asked.

"It's his," Daisy chirped from behind. "And yours when you get married."

Ruth's shocked gaze swung his way. "You didn't say you had a house. I thought you only had land for a farm."

Micah shrugged and drove the horse up to the back of the house, stopping in front of an old barn that would probably need to be taken down eventually. He locked the buggy in place and climbed down. He lifted his sister out, and she began to make her way toward the picnic table.

"Actually," he called after her, "I was thinking we could take our snack by the stream."

"Yay!" Daisy shouted. "I love the frogs there."

Micah turned back for Ruth, but she had already stepped down and was coming around the rear of the buggy. She walked right by him and headed toward the back steps of the house. Micah retrieved the picnic basket and watched her approach the back door. She peered in through the window with her hand over her eyes.

"You can go in, you know," he said. "The key's under the mat."

She looked down at her feet. "It is? Isn't that dangerous? What if someone breaks in?"

Micah looked around at the vast hills that surrounded them. There was no sign of any other living being, and the only sound was the swish of the tall grasses blowing. "The Englisch cars don't even come out here. There's no reason for them to. The road has no outlet. And even if someone did break in, it's empty. Mr. Zook's furniture and belongings were divided up and shared among the community."

Ruth bent to retrieve the key and then opened the door. "You coming?" she asked.

"Nee," Micah's response was quick and sure.

She paused for a moment, then disappeared inside, pulling the screen door silently closed behind her. Micah stayed put while she took a look around. He wondered what she was thinking. Did she like the place?

What did it matter if she did?

After five minutes, she came back out, locked the place up, and put the key back in its place. She walked down the steps and right by him without a word.

"And?" He followed as she trailed after Daisy, who was, in her excitement, already halfway to the stream. "What did you think?"

There was no answer. No sound, either, but the soft sound of the grass brushing against her skirt.

"Ruth, why aren't you talking to me? Did I do something wrong?" Maybe, Micah thought, he shouldn't have brought her to the house. He knew there wasn't any point to it. "Please, talk to me."

She stopped and turned abruptly. "Talk to you? What am I supposed to say? Since my parents died, I haven't had a home. Then I met you and thought we were alike in this. Me, without a home. You, having to live with a family that doesn't understand you or accept you for who you are." She flung her arm wide toward the house. "Now I see you have a home, a real home of your own. And you want to leave it all behind? I would give anything to have such a thing. As it is, all I see are classified ads for small studio apartments I can't even afford. But you—you have all of this?" She turned in a circle to take it all in. Micah knew it was a good piece of property.

"It will go to Paul, and he'll be happy here." Micah walked up to her and reached for her hand. "Komm. Let's go to the stream. I told you, we need to talk." Ruth let him lead the way, but he caught her looking over her shoulder a couple of times. Did she want to stay here? Like . . . forever? "We need to stick to the plan, Ruth," he said sternly. "In fact, we need to push the timing up."

She tripped in the grass. He caught her before she fell. "But we can't," she said helplessly. "I agreed to help Teacher Frannie for two weeks."

"It can't happen. Paul knows."

Ruth's eyes widened. "He knows who I am?"

"Nee, but he knows you're not Rachel Miller. Not the Ohio Rachel Miller, anyway. He doesn't know your real name."

"Ach, Micah." Ruth stared at him. "Will he tell your parents?"

Micah smiled at her use of the Amish phrase. "He said he wouldn't, but he'll only give us a couple days. I told him that we have a plan and will make everything right. The first thing we need to do is find you a place."

Her shoulders sank. "I don't have much money saved up, and I don't know how long it will take me to find another job. I found one cheap room in a boardinghouse that might work, but that's it. I suppose I could take that for now. It's better than nothing."

Micah glanced back at the house. A flash of her living there crossed his mind, but he knew he couldn't rent her the place. Not when making things right involved giving it to Paul.

"We'll figure something out," he assured her. "Let's plan to go see the boardinghouse tomorrow after school. I'll take you there."

"All right. Danki."

When they reached the stream, Micah spread out the blanket for them and Daisy to sit on. The little girl joined them, and he opened the basket and passed around the strudel.

Silence fell around them as they bit into the sweet pastry and relished his mother's cooking for a few minutes.

"I hope I can become as *gut* of a cook as Mamm one day." Ruth swiped at the apple crumbs on her lips.

Once again Micah noticed her use of the term. He wondered if Ruth was beginning to see his mother as her own. Was Mamm filling a void in Ruth's life?

What if she couldn't bring herself to leave as they'd planned?

The absurd idea turned his stomach, and he tossed his strudel back into the basket. "We should get going." He stood up.

"But we just got here," Daisy complained. "Let me at least catch one frog. Pleeeease!"

"Let her," Ruth whispered. "You're mad at me about something. Not her."

"I'm not mad at you." His denial sounded weak, and Ruth's raised eyebrows showed him that she didn't believe him.

"Go ahead, Daisy," Micah said. "Ten minutes, though. I do need to get back. I have some things to do." *Like start packing.*

Daisy moved closer to the rocks by the stream. As soon as she was out of earshot, he said, "I'm worried you're becoming too attached to my family, and maybe even to the Amish life. We're both supposed to leave. You'll get your apartment, and I'll head to Nashville. That was the plan. But if you don't want to leave, then I'll just have to disappear alone into the night. If we left together as planned and said we were moving to another community in your state, or you decided to return to the Englisch world, they would accept that I would go with you, as divorce is not allowed. In that situation, they would be hurt. But if I go alone, they will be crushed. Please, Ruth, please stick to the plan."

"I am," she said, a bit too loudly. In a quieter voice, she said, "It's just that I promised Frannie, and Daisy made such good headway on her math today. I really can help the children with my knowledge of math. But I promise. It will only be for two weeks. After that, I'll leave with you and go to my own place, just like we planned."

Micah released a deep breath he hadn't realized he was holding. "*Gut.* Danki. I'll tell Paul and hope I can hold him off for a couple weeks. You worried me for a few moments."

"I'm sorry." She smiled at Daisy, who was gleefully holding up a frog. "*Gut* job, sweetie!"

Micah studied Ruth's profile. He could clearly see the love she felt for his sister in her expression. Her feelings were genuine. He wondered if, when he took her from here, she would feel as though she was losing a family all over again.

Micah hated the remorse that reared up in him. They had to stick to the plan. That was all there was to it. He had a dream to pursue. A new thought came to him then.

But what about Ruth's dream?

The question caused him to jump to his feet. "It's time to go."

"But it hasn't been ten minutes yet," Daisy whined.

"Now," Micah said sternly.

Daisy flinched at his tone, and Ruth stood up and went to her. She spoke softly to Daisy and helped her put the frog back in the water, on some leaves. The frog hopped right off and crossed the stream. Micah had the blanket balled up in his arms and the basket in his hand when they turned back. The gesture was meant to tell them that he intended to leave immediately, without any more delays.

Ruth assisted Daisy as she walked, and Micah's heart sank as the two of them passed him in exactly the same way Ruth had walked past him earlier.

In total silence.

Ruth sat beside Micah for the ride home, but something between them had changed. The comfortable companionship they had effortlessly enjoyed since meeting at the bar had flitted away. She was afraid that he would take anything she said the wrong way. He probably thought she was going to back out of their plan.

And what if she did?

When Micah pulled up to Connie's house, Ruth remained in her seat. "Micah," she started, but she didn't know how to tell him about her change of heart. She also had to be careful with her words, as Daisy might overhear her. "I love your family very much." She looked at him, hoping he would see that she was incapable of intentionally hurting them. "And I loved helping at the school today."

He faced her and took her hand in his. His fingers were warm from working the reins. "Two weeks is all I can give you," he said in a low voice. "I'm sorry. It's time. I'll pick you up tomorrow after school to go see the place. And Ru—Rachel . . ."

They both glanced back at Daisy, but the child was staring at Connie's house.

Micah continued, "My family loves you too. But I suppose I should have known they would." He squeezed her hand, and she squeezed back. If only they could freeze this moment. "What's not to love?" he said with a sad smile. The two of them stared at each other for a moment, knowing time was short. It seemed to Ruth that he was about to say something more, and she leaned in close to him.

"Paul!" Daisy shouted just then, causing Ruth and Micah to separate and glance at the house.

Paul stepped from the front door and sauntered their way. He came around the passenger side but didn't offer a hand to help Ruth down. He stood back in silence, waiting to take her seat as soon as she vacated it.

Ruth released Micah's hand and climbed out of the buggy so Paul could climb up. He settled into the buggy facing forward and didn't say a word to her.

"I'll see you tomorrow, Daisy," Ruth said. She nodded at Micah. "Give my best to your parents."

Paul made a scoffing noise under his breath but said nothing.

Something felt off with him. Ruth supposed his disgruntled demeanor had to do with the fact that he knew she wasn't the real Rachel Miller. She stepped back. "*Gut*-bye, Paul."

No reply.

Micah flicked the reins and turned the buggy around in the road, and then he pulled away, leaving Ruth behind. She wondered if Paul had told Connie what he knew. Maybe he had already told everyone. Maybe she didn't even have two weeks before she had to go.

She drew in a deep breath and let it out slowly, and then she made her way to the front door, opened it, and stepped inside quietly. There was no sign of Connie. Ruth walked through to the kitchen and saw the woman coming in the back door holding two tomatoes.

"Welcome home. How was your first day at the schoolhouse?" Connie spoke as if Ruth had announced herself.

"How did you know I was here?"

"I heard the buggy leave. And you're not as quiet as you think." Connie smiled and went to the counter to wash the tomatoes. "I'm making a sandwich. Are you hungry? I thought you would stay at my sister's for dinner, so it's nothing fancy, I'm afraid."

"A sandwich is fine. It's perfect, actually." How she would miss this woman. "How can I help?"

"Nonsense. You worked all day with the young ones. Go get freshened up, and I'll have a plate ready for you."

Ruth raced up to Connie and threw her arms around her.

Connie hesitated only a moment before she hugged Ruth back. "What's gotten into you? Is everything all right?" she asked.

Ruth wished she could tell the woman how much she would miss her. "I'm *gut*. I actually loved today so much."

"Ach, that's wunderbaar! And for certain sure, the children loved you."

"I think so."

"*Gut*. Now go. I'm famished." Connie gave Ruth one more squeeze and released her.

Ruth made her way to her bedroom but found her door wide open. She paused, trying to remember if she had left it that way in her rush to leave that morning. She supposed it was possible, but then she saw that her closet was also open and her purse lay on the bed.

Her Englisch purse—nothing an Amish woman would ever have. Especially with her Englisch wallet with driver's license inside.

Her wallet was also open.

Ruth looked back toward the kitchen where Connie bustled around. Ruth laughed off the idea immediately. Connie would never do such a thing. But someone else would. Someone *had*.

Paul.

Paul, who wouldn't even look at her outside . . . because he now knew she had never been Amish. This morning, he'd only known that she wasn't really Rachel Miller. Now he knew she was, and had always been, an Englischer.

Things had just gone from bad to worse. There was no way he wasn't telling his family everything tonight. Would they even let her say goodbye?

"Connie!" Ruth ran out to the kitchen. "Connie, I have to leave. I have to go to Micah's house. I have to talk to his parents."

"About what, dear?" Connie placed the plates on the table and turned her way. She wiped her hands on her apron.

But how to tell her?

"Paul was in my room."

"Whatever for? Are you sure?"

"Ja, he must have gone in there when you were out in the garden. Connie, he went through my belongings."

"Nee, ach, nee." Connie reached one hand to the back of a kitchen chair and stretched the other out to her. "Komm, child."

Ruth ran to her and held her hand. "Connie, there's something I have to tell you. I feel awful."

"I know, dear. I know you're Englisch."

"What? You do? H-how? When?"

"From the first moment you set foot in my house. I hugged you to confirm my suspicions and felt the fabric of your clothes. I knew in an instant. But my sister did not. I don't know how she missed it. I suppose they were just so happy to have you in their lives."

Her words only made Ruth feel worse. She dropped into a chair beside Connie. "I can't believe this. I can't believe you knew, and I can't believe my relationship with Mamm and Daed is about to end. I didn't even get to say goodbye."

"Why is your relationship about to end?"

It was inevitable that they would send her away. Ruth couldn't fathom how Connie could come to any other conclusion. "Because Paul is probably telling them right now."

"You don't know that. And so what if he does? If my sister and her husband don't realize how special you are, then they don't deserve a *gut*-bye. Simple as that. Besides, do you really want to go?"

Tears sprung to Ruth's eyes. "Ach, Connie, I don't. I want to stay forever, but I promised Micah I would help him."

"Help him by marrying him? Then you can stay."

"Nee." Ruth closed her eyes. Could she break Micah's confidence with Connie? "I came to help him . . . leave the Amish."

Connie exhaled and slumped back in her chair. Her face grew pale. "I don't believe it. I thought you . . . I thought you would make everything better. I thought you truly belonged here and would be what Micah needed to be content. I thought you loved us. But it was all a lie?"

"I do love you!" Ruth jumped up and wrapped her arms around Connie from behind her chair. "That's the problem. I love you all so much. I even love Paul and understand his fear of losing his brother. The pain it will cause the whole community. I love being Amish. I don't ever want to leave. You're my family. My true family." Ruth dropped her forehead onto Connie's shoulder and began to weep. "I can't lose you."

"But you also feel obligated to Micah and his plan to leave forever."

Ruth sniffed and nodded. "What do I do? Tell me."

"Well, it's always best to start with asking for forgiveness. Admitting to the wrong will set the correct path in motion. We can go talk to Bishop Yoder tonight." Connie reached up to Ruth's face and caressed her damp cheek. "And if you're serious about staying, a baptism can be discussed as well."

"What about Micah? Aunt Connie, I think I love him. Nee. I know I love him."

Connie sighed. "Letting go will be the hardest thing you ever do. Believe me. But Micah will have to find his way on his own. None of us can walk another's journey. We can only walk our own."

Ruth felt lighter already. She did not have to bear the weight of her and Micah's lie any longer. "Aunt Connie, my name is Ruth Griffin, and I know my journey has led me right to this community and I'm meant to stay here . . . forever."

Connie patted her cheek. "Welcome home, Ruth."

CHAPTER SEVENTEEN

The next morning, Connie agreed to join Ruth at the Stolzfus house, where Ruth planned to come clean with the family. The evening before at Bishop Yoder's house had changed her life forever. The bishop's offer of forgiveness, and the understanding he showed her, only proved to her that her decision to become Amish, truly and permanently, was the right choice for her. But she still needed to seek the forgiveness of every Stolzfus family member. She also needed to talk with Micah to tell him that their plan was over.

And to tell him that she loved him. She only hoped that she would have a chance to pull him aside and tell him before she spoke to the others.

When Ruth stepped inside the kitchen, she noticed that all the girls were abuzz with excitement. They all sat around the table, which was laden with craft materials.

"We're making Frannie's wedding decorations. Komm, help us!" Daisy shouted. "Yours will be next."

Leah shushed her daughter. "Let the couple make that announcement when it's time." She turned to her sister. "Connie, so lovely to have you this morning. I have tea on the woodstove. Sit, and let me get you a cup." Leah pushed back from the table.

"Actually, this isn't a pleasure visit. We have something to discuss with you." Connie's serious tone had a dampening effect on the room, which a moment before had practically crackled with excitement.

Leah looked at her girls. "We'll finish this later. Go—"

"Nee," Ruth interrupted her. "They need to stay. In fact, everyone should be here for this. Since you're all still showing me acceptance, I can only assume Paul hasn't told you what he learned yesterday." Surely it was only a matter of time before he did so. There wasn't a moment to waste.

Leah sat back down. "Learned? Learned about what?"

Ruth gave her a nervous look. "If you don't mind, I would like to wait until everyone is here and do this only once."

Leah's brow furrowed. "Okay. Sadie, go get your father and brothers from the barn."

The teenager jumped up and ran to the door, letting the screen door slam behind in her hustle. After a few moments, she returned with only her Daed.

"Paul and Micah are already out in the fields," Jacob said. "What's this all about? Why are you taking me away from my morning work?" Ruth's heart sank at his words. She wouldn't have a chance to talk with Micah first after all. But there was nothing to be done about it. Connie had gotten the ball rolling, and there was no pausing it now.

Leah said to her *Mann*, "Rachel has something to tell us."

Jacob smiled. "Is that so?"

Ruth realized that Jacob believed she was about to make her and Micah's wedding announcement. Guilt caused her to feel a plummeting sensation in her stomach.

She needed to tell them her real name. But she didn't feel comfortable breaking this news alone. She had wanted to have

Micah beside her when she did it. She could only hope and pray that the others would accept her apology. She prayed that this dear Amish family would be willing to forgive her and not hold her sins against her forever.

Forever.

The idea of having nearly become a part of this family brought tears to her eyes. She had wanted that more than anything. The girls at the table all sat quietly. Sadie's voice trailed off to silence until they were all looking at her with concern.

Jacob beamed her way. "Ach, what is it, Dochder? Don't leave us in suspense."

More tears streamed from Ruth's eyes. Being called *daughter* by Jacob was more than she could have ever hoped for or dreamed of. But she also knew she didn't deserve this family. She was only there now as a result of her own deception.

"There's something you all need to know, and it's not about a wedding."

Jacob frowned. "Go ahead. We're listening."

Ruth didn't want to lie anymore. Her gaze drifted to the window. If only Micah would come in from the fields for some reason. She chose her words carefully, keeping as close to the truth as possible.

"I found Micah to be a safe refuge when I first met him. I honestly wasn't expecting to find him attractive, but I did." It wasn't a total lie. She had never thought she would be attracted to an Amish man. "More importantly, he had a trustworthy face. And I appreciated that more than anything." Ruth thought about the last, horrifying relationship she'd had before Micah, which had been a source of nightmares even before Taylor's death. "I knew Micah would never hurt me."

Leah reached for Ruth's hand and squeezed it. Her eyes were now filling with tears, just as Ruth's had. "We are so blessed to have you, Rachel. I have to admit, when you arrived, I worried that this might have been a mistake for my son. Your ways were not like our ways. But now I see that you are everything we could have hoped for. I do not doubt that you and Micah will have a wonderful marriage." A worried expression came over her face. "I do hope you're not here to tell us you decided not to pursue marriage. If I had anything to do with that decision, I am sorry. Forgive me for doubting in the beginning. If I could go back to scold myself, I would."

"Nee, your concern was valid, and yet you decided to accept me immediately. I will never forget that." Ruth looked around the table. "I love you all so much. You're all so wunderbaar. I want my home someday to be filled with so much love, just like this one." She directed her words at the whole room.

Leah made a little snorting sound. "You'll get there. Don't rush it. Before you know it, your rooms will be filled with children, and then you will be planning *their* weddings."

Ruth frowned and fidgeted with the side seam of her dress while Leah still held her other hand. "Just a few weeks ago, I would have never let myself even dream of such a thing."

The sound of crunching gravel drifted through the window screens. Daisy turned in her chair to look out the window behind her.

"It's a taxi car!" she announced to everyone. "Who could be visiting us in a taxi?"

Leah stood up and walked to the door. "Stay here, children. Daed and I will see to this. I'm sure it's nothing to be concerned about." Leah and Jacob walked outside. Ruth watched from the window as the car pulled up and stopped in front of them.

The children inside the house all crammed beside Ruth to watch through the window. Connie turned her head and sat in concerned silence.

Who could be arriving at their door?

First an older Amish man got out of one side of the car, and then an Amish woman of approximately the same age climbed out on the other side. She held the door for another person in the car who seemed to be taking their time.

"They're Amish," Sadie announced. "But I've never seen them before."

"I wonder who they are," Daisy said with her hands on the window ledge.

Ruth didn't have the faintest idea. All she knew was her repentance had been put on hold, and that only made her feel sicker. She wanted to get this over with. Bishop Yoder had offered to meet her here, but Ruth thought it best to make her confession alone. Now, she wished she had taken him up on his offer.

The Amish man frowned and poked his head into the car. A moment later, a young Amish woman stepped out. Brown hair poked out from beneath her Kapp, and she was sturdily built. She kept her head down as she followed the Amish man over to the Stolzfuses' house. The older Amish woman followed behind them. As the man spoke to Micah's parents, their faces took on expressions of concern.

Leah clutched at her chest, and her knees buckled.

Sadie said, "Something's wrong. This is not *gut* news."

Then Leah looked toward the house, and through the window, she caught Ruth's gaze. She nodded and crooked a finger at Ruth, indicating that she should come out there.

Ruth stepped away from the window, her head pounding with thoughts about what this development undoubtedly meant. She made her way toward the door and, with quiet steps, walked what felt like her last mile. A quick glance toward the fields showed nothing but swaying grass beyond the fence. Micah could be gone for hours.

She would have to face her sins alone.

Long before Ruth reached the group, she had figured out who they were. When she stopped in front of the young Amish girl, Ruth knew who she was looking at.

The girl appeared to be annoyed, but she didn't say anything to Ruth. In fact, she did not meet anyone's gaze, choosing instead to focus on something in the distance, beyond them all. The man did all the talking.

"We are hoping the wedding can still occur as planned," he said.

Leah's jaw was tight. "That will be a decision my son will have to make." She looked to Ruth. "This is Rachel Miller, the girl Micah is to marry. But I suppose you already knew that."

"Ja," Ruth said. "I can explain."

Without glancing her way, Jacob replied, "Do not bother. There will be a wedding. But it will not be yours."

Micah and Paul led the workhorses back to the barn just before lunchtime. Paul had been eerily quiet ever since they had left for the fields after breakfast. In fact, he had been more silent than usual ever since Micah brought Ruth back to Connie's the night before.

Finally, Micah couldn't take it any longer. "Can you be happy for me at all?" he asked.

Paul shook his head. "With any other girl, I would. But not her. She's not who you think she is, Bruder. You've been duped into believing she's some innocent person. I hate to tell you this, but she's only pretending to be Amish. She's Englisch, and she's wanted—"

"I know this," Micah cut him off. "I asked her to do it."

Paul nearly tripped over his feet. "You can't be serious. Why would you do such a thing? There are plenty of Amish girls who would have married you."

"Marriage wasn't the original plan. It never was. If I had wanted to marry anyone, I would have married someone in our community years ago." Micah started walking again with his horse and plow.

Paul stayed planted in one spot with a confused expression on his face. After a few moments, he clambered to catch up. "So, you're not going to marry this woman?"

Micah's frustration had reached its limit. He turned to his brother. "No! Ruth and I will not be married."

Saying the words out loud stirred up a melancholy feeling within him, but that melancholy, he knew, was something he would simply have to get used to. "The house and farm are yours. I wish you many happy years there. I won't be around to see what you do with the place. That should only make you even happier." Micah picked up his steps to put distance between them.

Paul chased after him, kicking up the loose, overturned dirt. "You don't get it! I wanted you to get married because then I knew you would never leave! I didn't want the farm! I wanted you in our lives forever!"

Paul continued to shout at Micah's back. "Do you think I didn't know that you longed to be part of the Englisch world? We all knew it. When you brought this woman home, I knew she wasn't the answer to you staying with us. I knew she wasn't really Amish, and all I could think was when she went back to her world, you would go with her. Please, Micah, I don't want to lose my big Bruder. Please send her away and stay with us."

Micah stopped and took in his brother's confession. So much made sense now. "Rachel—"

"Stop with the lies," Paul said firmly. "You know her name is not Rachel. Her name is Ruth Griffin. And I beg you to send her back."

"If she goes back, I go with her!" The words spilled from Micah's mouth without a second thought. Paul's stunned expression as soon as Micah said them matched how Micah felt. But the shock only lasted a few seconds, because suddenly, Micah recognized the truth. How had he missed it before? "I've been so blind," he whispered.

Paul squinted at him. "Why? What is this woman to you?"

Micah hesitated. He'd known he cared for Ruth, but those words failed to capture the scope of his feelings. He cared for his family as well, but he had been willing to leave them for what he loved most.

"Ach," he said, "I think I love her. Nee, I know I love her. I don't know how it happened or when, but ja, I love Ruth Griffin." Saying it aloud felt freeing. His lips widened into a huge smile. He tore his straw hat from his head and tunneled his fingers through his hair. "I need to tell her." He looked at the house in the distance and started moving toward it.

"Wait!" Paul ran along behind him, trying to catch up. "Are you serious?"

"Ja! For certain sure, I love Ruth Griffin!" Micah yelled from the top of his lungs. He dropped the reins to his plow horse and began to run toward his love. For years, he had hesitated to run toward his dream of being a professional musician. But today, there was no hesitancy in his steps.

"Micah! I have to tell you something," Paul shouted. "I made another phone call. I didn't know you loved her. I just wanted her sent back to where she came from."

Paul's words registered just as Micah caught sight of a taxi pulling out of the driveway and disappearing down the street. *Sent back?*

Paul was shouting in Micah's wake. "I'm sorry, Bruder!" he called loudly. "I didn't know!"

Micah didn't want to hear any more. He only knew that he needed to catch up to Ruth, wherever she had gone. Wherever she had been sent off to. And this time, he knew he wouldn't waver. If getting Ruth back meant he would have to leave his family this very day, he would leave immediately and never look back.

He raced toward the fence and cleared it in one jump. As he neared the house, he noticed his siblings were all standing outside. He stopped in front of Sadie and Daisy. "Is Ruth here?" He bent over and tried to catch his breath.

"Who?" Sadie asked.

His heart raced, and he was short of breath. "Her name is Ruth. Not Rachel. Just tell me where she went."

Sadie's expression conveyed her uncertainty and shock. "She's in the house."

So he wasn't too late after all. A wave of relief fell over him. "Ach, thank Gött." He ran for the porch.

"But Micah," Sadie called after him, "she's not alone."

Micah barely registered the words. He had one goal and one goal only, and that was to tell Ruth that he loved her. He burst into the kitchen . . . and froze.

There at the table were the real Rachel Miller's parents, from Ohio. Their presence in his home confused him. As he looked around the table, his attention fell on Rachel Miller herself. She looked as angry as she had the first time he showed up at her door.

"What are you doing here?" he asked her.

"Rachel is here to marry you, as planned," Mamm said from the head of the table. Daed stood behind Mamm with his hand on her shoulder. The two of them were a perfect picture of solidarity.

"Nee," Micah said. "Where is Ruth?"

"Ruth? Is that her name?" Daed asked. "It would have been nice to know that from the beginning. Lying is unacceptable. How did you ever think you could keep such a thing secret?"

"Where is she? Ruth!" Micah raced into the living room to search for her. The room was empty. "Ruth!" Was she even still here? Maybe Sadie had been wrong. Maybe she had been in the taxi after all, and his siblings just didn't know it.

Then he heard a soft voice. "I'm right here."

Micah looked up and saw Ruth standing at the top of the stairs. She had tears streaming down her cheeks. He raced up the steps two at a time until he had her wrapped up in his arms and pulled tight against his chest. "Ach, *Lieb*. I'm so sorry. I should have been here."

Ruth buried her face into the crook of his neck. He could feel her hot tears against his skin, and he gently pulled her head up so that he could wipe them away with his thumbs. The longing look in her eyes scared him. Surely Ruth didn't think he would choose the woman in the kitchen. Did she not know how he felt about her?

But then again, how could she? He'd never told her. Until just minutes ago, not even he had known just how he felt.

"I'll fix this," he told her. "Do not worry. This changes nothing, Ruth. We will still be married."

Her head lifted quickly. "We will? For real?"

"I mean, if you'll have me. I would be so honored to be your Mann."

She shook her head, which he still held gently with his hands. "Your parents said you will marry Rachel. There's nothing we can do."

"Then I'll leave with you, just like we always planned."

"Nee," she said. "I won't let you. I won't break up a family. I can't be the cause of such turmoil. And there's something you need to know. I've done something that can't be undone, and I honestly don't want to undo it."

"Whatever it is, we'll figure it out, together." Micah dropped his forehead to hers. "I love you, Ruth. Do you understand me? I love you. You would be all the family I would ever need. We would go wherever you wanted."

"I only want to stay here." Her lips trembled. "But Micah, our lies have ruined everything. We should have realized all this would hurt so many people."

He smiled at her loving heart. She always thought of others before herself. It was why she agreed to help him to begin with. "If I had known how much I would love you, I would have brought you, Ruth Griffin, home with me, and you would never have had to pretend to be anyone but yourself." He frowned. "I'm so sorry I made you pretend to be Rachel Miller. Can you ever forgive me? We can make this right, now."

She reached up and covered his hands where he still held her face. Slowly, she gripped his fingers and tried to pull them away. He held fast, not wanting to hear her next words. "It's too late. Micah, I have to leave this home. You have to figure out how to go on and . . . and marry Rachel as you agreed."

"Never. You will be the only Fraa I will ever have. Listen to me. I love you. Ruth, I'm *in* love with you."

As he spoke, Ruth's eyes grew guarded, and her head tilted as she studied him. He could see his words were finally sinking in. Their love wasn't a platonic love any longer, and they both knew it.

Micah forced himself to ask the question that had to be asked, no matter how much he feared her response. "Do you love me, Ruth? I mean, really love me, the way a man and woman pledged to marry should love one another?"

He held his breath while imploring her with his eyes to say yes. When she shook her head, he felt a tightness in his chest.

"Micah, your bride is sitting downstairs," Ruth said. "Please, don't make this harder than it has to be. You have to stay here with your family. But don't worry about me. Gött is leading me to my place. I've spoken to Bishop Yoder, and I will be fine."

He leaned back so that he could take in her whole face. "You went to Bishop Yoder? But you're not Amish. Why would you—"

She pulled his hands from her face, breaking their connection in an instant, and whispered, "I have to go." She moved to pass him on the stairs, and he reached for her arm to stop her.

"Please don't," he said. Panic threaded his voice.

Sadie shouted from downstairs, "Another car is here!"

Ruth locked gazes with him. He asked her, "Did you call for a cab?"

"Nee," she said. "All I did was run upstairs and hide, like the coward I am."

A jolt of anger caused him to clench his jaw. "You are not a coward," he said in a ragged voice. "Don't ever say that again."

Sadie yelled again, "It's an Englisch woman named Kathy. She says she's here for Ruth." Micah felt as though his life was spiraling out of control.

"My sister," Ruth whispered harshly. "What is *she* doing here? How did she find me?"

"You never told her where you were, right?"

"Never."

Micah took Ruth's hand. "Komm. We'll find out what she wants." He led her down the stairs, but as they reached the bottom, Ruth pulled her hand from his grasp before anyone could see them touching.

She hurried ahead of him but stopped short when she saw the woman who stood at the back screen door.

"There you are." Kathy's words were filled with anger. "Do you have any idea what I've been going through because of you?"

"Nee, I don't," Ruth admitted, and Micah could hear the remorse in her voice. "I'm sorry, I should have told you where I was."

Kathy opened the screen door and stepped inside. She cringed at the sight of the people at the table and looked around the room. "What *is* this place? What in the world are you doing here?" she scoffed. Then she shook her head. "Never mind. It doesn't matter. Get in the car. I'm taking you back to Pittsburgh. The police have been looking for you. They've been camped out in front of my apartment for the last week, hoping to catch you."

"Catch me?" Ruth looked startled. She took in a sharp breath and stepped back into Micah. He put his arm around her and felt her trembling. "For what?"

"For murder. You killed a man, or had you forgotten that little detail while you were playing . . . *dress-up*?" Kathy flung a hand to reference Ruth's purple Amish dress.

Micah heard several of his family members gasp. Mamm let out a little cry that she stifled with her knuckles. "Micah, what have you done in bringing this woman to our home?" she asked.

"It's not what it sounds like." He spoke in a panicked rush, his tone pleading for his family to listen first before making a judgment.

"It's *exactly* what it sounds like," Kathy said. "An eyewitness has testified that they saw Ruth kill a man in the parking lot of the bar. Now, get in my car, Ruth, or the police will come to collect you. Is that what you want?"

Ruth gulped loudly and shook her head. She looked around the room, but no one would make eye contact with her. "Please, you must believe me. I never wanted to hurt any of you. I never wanted to hurt anyone."

No one said anything. Micah took her hand. "I'm going with you."

"No!" Three people protested at once: Mamm, Daed, and Ruth. But he would allow none of them to change his mind.

"I'm going with Ruth. Get used to it. All of you." He pulled Ruth from the house, following after Kathy. When they reached the car, he let Ruth get in the back first and then he climbed in after her.

"But I don't want you to come," Ruth protested as Kathy started the car.

Micah looked out the passenger window as Kathy drove away from the only home he'd ever known. He sat beside the woman of his heart, knowing that there was nowhere else he could choose to be, even though she didn't feel the same way about him.

"Yes, well," he said grimly, "if I've learned anything in these last few weeks, and even in these last few minutes, it's that we don't always get what we want."

CHAPTER EIGHTEEN

Ruth walked into the police station with Kathy right behind her, practically pushing her inside. It was painfully obvious that Kathy couldn't wait to see Ruth humiliated and booked for murder.

Murder.

The idea that she would intentionally kill someone was ridiculous. "I'm Ruth Griffin," she said to the officer at the front desk. "I've been told the police have some more questions to ask me."

"Come this way." The officer unlocked a door to the back of the station and led her through it.

"Ruth, I'll be right here," Micah said before the door closed on him.

"Go home, Micah." She tried to keep the emotion she felt from her voice. "Get away from all this. Go home and have a *gut* life."

The door shut before he could say anything else.

The officer left Ruth in an interview room where she sat for what seemed like over an hour. She practically chewed through her bottom lip. Her anxiety levels skyrocketed, and her breathing came in short bursts.

"Time to come clean, Miss Griffin," the officer said when he finally came back to question her. His name badge read Officer Franklin. "You have some explaining to do. When you were questioned the night of the killing, you neglected to share some pertinent information. Why didn't you tell us the victim had gotten you fired that day?"

Ruth's mouth went dry. When she shifted in her chair, she realized her body had gone numb. "I-I didn't think it was important, I guess." She licked her lips. She kept telling herself that she had nothing to worry about, but a glance at the mirror on the wall told her otherwise. Surely someone stood on the other side of the glass, watching. Were they waiting for her to say something to incriminate herself?

The officer leaned in. "Not important? Where I come from, a detail like that's called motive."

Suddenly, Ruth could feel the walls closing in on her. Her throat tightened as the gravity of the situation set in. "Why am I a suspect now, when I wasn't before? I told you everything that happened that night in the parking lot. Taylor attacked me. I was only trying to get away from him. I hit him with the microphone, and he fell back. But he got back up. He wasn't dead when I ran to the bus. Nothing's changed."

"Except, it has," Officer Franklin told her. "Everything has changed. We have sworn testimony from someone who saw you hit Taylor Williams twice: once to fend him off, and a second time after he was down. That second strike is what killed him. And your prints are all over the murder weapon."

"Well, of course they are!" Ruth said. "I just told you I was holding the microphone. But I know I only hit him once and then dropped the mic to the ground. I never hit him a second time."

"Save that argument for the judge." Officer Franklin stood and removed a pair of handcuffs from his belt. "Please stand, Miss Griffin."

Ruth tried to catch her breath. "Wait, please, there's been a mistake. Someone is lying. I didn't kill anyone."

"Stand up now," he said in a cool voice, "or I'll add another charge of resisting arrest."

"Resisting?" Ruth stared at him. "I came in here by choice."

"Stand up." The tone of his voice told her there was no room for negotiation.

Ruth did as she was told, and the officer turned her around to cinch her hands in the metal cuffs. He led her out of the room, and in what was the most humiliating moment Ruth had ever experienced, she was booked and fingerprinted. As the officer escorted her to a holding cell afterward, she thought of Micah. Was he still out in the waiting room? Or had he returned to his home and simple life, as she'd told him to?

"Please, can you check to make sure Micah Stolzfus has left? If he hasn't, tell him I said to go home and never come back. If that doesn't work, tell him I—tell him I don't love him. Tell him to marry Rachel. It's the honorable thing to do." Her voice cracked as she spoke the words that would sever her connection to the man that she would love forever.

"As far as I know, he's still out there. Your sister's long gone, though." The cell door slammed shut. Ruth trembled as a cold feeling fell over her.

She put a hand on one steel bar and slowly slumped to the concrete floor. As she rested her forehead on the bars, she remembered how it had felt to lean against Micah just a few hours earlier. But this was her life now. The only person she could count on was herself. This had been the case for a very long time.

How could she have forgotten that? She was in this mess because she had forgotten this fact and had allowed herself to trust Taylor's charming ways.

Now, Ruth would pay for years to come. And she would do it totally and utterly alone.

Micah found himself walking aimlessly around the city of Pittsburgh, remembering when he had been here last. Only a short time had passed since that night, but he had been forever changed.

Before Ruth versus after Ruth.

Before love versus after love.

He put a hand to his chest as the police officer's words played over and over in his head.

"She said to tell you that she doesn't love you."

As he made his way to the bus station, he squeezed the bridge of his nose to stop the tears that were threatening to spill. He needed another one-way ticket to somewhere.

But to where?

As he walked by the same bar where he had met Ruth, he saw the flashing karaoke sign that had lured him inside, forever changing his life. He had gone inside to pursue one love but had come out alongside his true love. Could he now return to that first love again?

He passed the bar and headed into the station. At the ticket counter, he grew tongue-tied when he thought about where to go. Places like Nashville and Los Angeles came to mind.

Whatever choice he made now, though, he would have to live with forever. Leave, and never have a family again, or return and dedicate himself to the Amish life, farm and all.

What, he wondered, would Ruth want for him?

She had told him to marry Rachel. He would do anything for Ruth, but this felt wrong. Why would she ask such a thing of him?

The answer came to him in an instant: because she loved his family. She had said so. She even loved Paul, who had constantly given her a hard time. Micah smiled, remembering how she held her own with them all and earned their love so quickly. Amish or not, Ruth Griffin fit in with his family even better than he did. It didn't feel right to go home and marry Rachel Miller instead of her.

Yet even before he answered the ticket attendant, Micah knew that was exactly what he would do. And he would do it for Ruth. He would do it for his family, whom he loved. Deep down inside, Micah had known the truth all along: when it came right down to it, he would never leave them.

Only the week before, he had arrived on Rachel Miller's doorstep, ready to meet his bride. And now, he would return to Lititz and marry her as planned.

"A one-way ticket to Lititz, please." He pulled his wallet from his pants pocket.

"That bus leaves in ten minutes. Are you ready to go?"

Micah swallowed hard. "Ja, I'm ready to go. I'm ready to do this." His voice cracked, but he kept his composure. Marrying Rachel Miller was the right and honorable thing to do, and he would do it, not because it was expected of him, but in order to keep the family together.

But what about Ruth? Micah knew that she didn't deserve to sit in a jail cell for a crime she didn't commit. And she didn't deserve to face this trial alone. But what could he do if she was just going to send him away? Ruth needed her family, and by that, he didn't mean Kathy, who had so cruelly rejected her. The only family Ruth had was his. But they, too, had rejected her today, and Micah doubted that they were ready to embrace her again.

Micah settled into his seat on the bus and leaned against the window. As the minutes passed, he watched the city lights disappear, and a cloak of country darkness fell over the vehicle. The glitz and glamour of city life slowly disappeared behind him, and the light of the heavenly stars lit up the sky, guiding Micah home. With each passing mile, he began to make a new plan, one that would involve everyone. He didn't know if anybody in his community would get on board, but he did know that Ruth Griffin had touched them all.

Micah would do as was expected of him.

But he would make sure that the others all knew what he expected of them as well.

CHAPTER NINETEEN

Ruth was all too eager to get out of her jail cell after spending the whole night there. She was brought to the courthouse the next morning and put into a room to wait. She'd barely slept and had spent most of the time since her arrest going through every detail she could remember from the night of Taylor's death. She was eager to meet her public defender so she could share what she knew.

"Ruth Griffin!" A short, round guard with a mustache called her name and opened the door. He brought her to a room, his keys clinking the whole way as he walked down a long corridor beside her. There, a blond man in his twenties with baby-fine facial hair and a loose-fitting suit was sitting at a table, looking over a file.

He glanced up when she sat down across from him, then he quickly looked back at the papers in front of him. His brow furrowed.

"Your file doesn't say that you're Amish. Forgive me, I didn't know."

Ruth glanced down at her purple dress. She still wore the same clothes she'd left Lititz in. Her Englisch clothes were still at Connie's house, hidden away in her closet. Ruth wondered how long it would be before someone found them. Probably years, she thought.

"I wasn't Amish the night at the bar. I've been living with a community in Lititz since. It's a long story, but I'd like to tell it to you. I really believe that if we explain things to the judge today, he'll see that this is all a big mistake. I didn't kill anyone. If Taylor died, someone else had to have done it."

"Whoa." The attorney raised his hands in the air. "You're getting way ahead of yourself. This is just an arraignment. You're not going to share any details with the judge today. Just your plea: guilty or not guilty."

But Ruth wanted this man to stick up for her. "I thought attorneys were a voice for their clients. Right now, that's what I need."

"Right now," the man said, waving a hand dismissively, "all I need is for you to tell me if you're guilty or not guilty. I don't want to hear any details. This is going to go very fast. You'll go in. You'll hear the charges that are being set against you. And you'll respond with guilty or not guilty. Then you'll close your mouth and wait for the judge's direction. He'll set your bail and schedule a date for you to return. It could be a week from now. It could be six months."

Ruth inhaled. "Six months? I have to stay in that jail cell for six months?" Ruth felt her heart pounding in her chest.

He shook his head and squinted at her. "No, of course not. You'll be moved to the city jail. After you make bail, you'll get out and go about your life until your court date."

"But . . . but what if I don't have anyone to pay for my bail?"

The attorney shrugged and held up his empty hands. "Then you might as well get comfy in your jail cell. Once we have your court date, we'll go over the details that I'll need to defend you."

In other words, she was on her own. Just as she'd known herself to be.

Ruth put her hand up. "If I could simply talk to the judge, I just know that I—"

"If you know what's good for you," he said sternly, "you will not say anything to the judge . . . except guilty or not guilty. Do you understand?"

"Ja. I understand." But Ruth didn't. All she knew was that she was so tired of not having a voice. She was so tired of feeling like everyone's doormat. She was so tired of feeling inconsequential, of never belonging. So tired of being pushed from one place to the next. From her home to her sister's apartment to Micah's house to a jail cell. When would all this moving around stop? Ruth couldn't help but think that it wouldn't stop until she spoke up for herself.

But could she do it?

"When do I go in front of the judge?" Ruth wondered if she would have the nerve to speak in her own defense if this defender wouldn't.

"Not until Tuesday. It's a long holiday weekend."

"Tuesday?" Her voice squeaked. Ruth shuddered at the prospect of spending the whole long weekend in her jail cell. She supposed it would give her time to prepare her words. She also realized that Micah would be likely married by Tuesday.

It pained her that they'd had to part so abruptly. They would now both have to endure hardships that were beyond their control. She prayed that Micah would not feel that his life had become a virtual prison.

And she prayed that she wouldn't be forced to spend her life in an actual one.

The whole community attended Micah's Monday night wedding. His family and community had transformed the barn for the ceremony, using the decorations that were supposed to be for

Frannie's nuptials. Benches were lined up as if it was a typical church day, but to Micah, the event felt more like a funeral. He half expected to see a body lying in state. He supposed, though, that his life was the dead body.

He had spent the last four days getting to know Rachel Miller. The real Rachel Miller, who would become his Fraa for life. He supposed she was nice enough. Somehow they'd gotten past her initial anger and annoyance, and she'd been respectful and kind ever since. He appreciated her gumption—after all, she had turned him down the first time they met. He respected that about her, and he also respected her decision to go through with the wedding.

They had found their stories to be similar. They were both bound by duty to find a mate. They both understood that it was time for them to start a family of their own. The night before, they had sat together in this barn and agreed to go through with the wedding that had been planned by their parents. Rachel was kind enough not to remind him that his heart belonged to another, and stated their marriage would be one of friendship. He asked her if he could kiss her, and she agreed. The kiss was fine, though it was nothing like he'd felt when he kissed Ruth. Rachel was sweet, and Micah decided that he would be content with sweet. He knew deep down Ruth would always be the love of his life, but that he would not let that stop him from being a *gut* Mann to Rachel.

As Micah stood in front of the community and waited for Rachel and his sisters to enter the barn, Paul stood beside him in the heavy silence. He had been quite morose since the day Ruth left. Guilt obviously weighed on him, and Micah knew he couldn't let that go on.

"Calling Rachel's family was the right thing to do," he told his brother quietly. "I forgive you."

Paul's brow furrowed. "I only called Rachel's family once. That's not who I called the second time," he whispered back and looked through the crowd beneath his lashes.

Micah tilted his head in confusion. "Who did you call?"

"I called the place where Ruth lived. Her sister answered, and I told her where she could find her." Paul dropped his head. Micah's mind whirled as he tried to make sense of this.

Micah drew in his breath in shock. He struggled inwardly with his initial impulse to extend forgiveness to Paul. "It's because of you that she's in jail right now? She did nothing wrong."

"I didn't know, Bruder." Paul's head still hung low, remorse in his voice. "I made the phone call and was told she was wanted for murder. I didn't know that you knew, and I didn't know that she didn't do it. Are you sure she didn't?"

"Ja, positive. I was there. She didn't kill anyone, and now she's being framed. She doesn't deserve this. She deserves . . ." Micah looked around at all the people Ruth loved so openly. "She deserves to have her family by her side. Her true family."

The back door opened, and Rachel walked into the barn followed by his sisters. She made her way to him as the girls sang behind her. She wore a pretty blue dress, and her hair was done perfectly. She caught his eye and offered him a simple smile. Then her gaze drifted to Paul, and her eyes filled with concern. Micah took one look at Paul's downtrodden face and thought he understood why. She probably wondered what Paul was so upset about. She had no idea that if it weren't for Paul's actions, she wouldn't even be getting married. As she made her way to the front, Micah knew that he could not marry her until Ruth was free.

"Stop," he told her. He looked around the barn at all the questioning faces pointed his way. "This wedding can't go on right now."

People sat up straighter and looked around the room. Whispers ensued.

Micah continued, "Not while Ruth sits in jail. She loved you all. And if you are honest, you will admit that you loved her too. Your children adore her. Think about how, in just a few hours, they came to trust her. We should be taking our direction from them. They are wiser than those of us who should know better."

People looked away. Some looked down at their laps or at the walls.

"Be honest," Micah persisted. "She is one of us. We are a family. We have no right to go on as if she didn't come into our lives. She needs her family right now more than anything. But instead, we all are sitting here, acting as if she never existed."

Mamm spoke from the front row of the barn. "What would you like us to do?" She wore a frown, and Micah could see she was not angry but brokenhearted.

"What you would do for any of your children who needed you," Micah said gently. "Be there for her."

"I caused this," Paul interjected. "I turned her in because I didn't believe in her. But I trust Micah, and if he says she's innocent, then she is surely innocent." He looked around at the crowd of people who were hanging on his every word. "I called on Friday to check on her."

Micah turned to him. He'd had no idea that Paul had done this. "What did you find out? Why didn't you tell me?"

"Guilt, I suppose. Maybe I didn't want to make things even worse. The important thing is, Ruth is being arraigned tomorrow morning at the courthouse." Paul looked out over the crowd. "I'm going to be there. This is my fault. I need to go support her."

Mamm stood up. "I'm going with you."

Connie stood up beside her. "I love Ruth as if she was my own child, and in many ways, she is. I will be with her through all of this."

Tears sprang to Micah's eyes. As he watched, one by one, people of his community admitted their love for Ruth and vowed to go to the courthouse. He turned to Rachel. "I can't marry you today," he said. "Not until Ruth is free. I promise I will marry you immediately after."

Rachel nodded. "I do not know your Ruth, but I will be there too."

Paul smiled at Rachel. "You are so kind, Rachel."

The girl blushed and dropped her gaze to the floor. Micah eyed them both for a moment, and then Paul looked at him with a new look of determination. "I'm sorry, Bruder. I don't know if our presence will help Ruth's case, but I do hope it shows her that we all love her."

Micah shot him an astonished stare. "I thought you hated her."

Paul shook his head. "I only feared she would take you away from us, when in truth she is the one who brought you home. For that, I will always be indebted to her."

Micah shook his head. "She would not want you to be. And just so you know, she loves you too."

Paul's eyes shone with tears. "I feel so guilty. If I hadn't gotten involved, she would be standing here with you right now."

Micah put a hand on his brother's arm. "It was only a matter of time before this case caught up to her. You did what was right. You were only trying to protect me, and she knows that."

Paul swallowed hard and looked out at the crowd. "We can leave tonight. I checked, and there's a bus that will get us to the courthouse by morning. It's practically empty and can fit about forty people. Those who are coming, be ready to go in a few hours. Those who will stay behind to care for the animals and children, please start to prepare."

Daisy shouted, "I want to go see Ruth! Please let me come too! I love her!"

Micah looked her way. "Absolutely, you will be there." He slapped his brother on the back and pulled him into a tight embrace. "Thank you, Bruder. I couldn't do this without you."

CHAPTER TWENTY

Ruth was brought from the police station early Tuesday morning and held in another jail cell at the courthouse. Here she waited with other people who were also awaiting arraignment. Ruth found a spot on a long bench and stared out the bars at a blank wall on the other side. She prayed that her public defender would speak up for her, even though he'd said that this court proceeding wasn't the time for that. She didn't know much about the judicial system, but she knew enough to recognize that it could take years for a trial to happen. And since she couldn't make bail, she would be waiting in a cell all that time.

Not that anyone would miss her.

Ruth prepared herself to face the judge alone. Would the fact that she had no one to vouch for her undermine her credibility?

The cell door opened, and the guard gave a nod that told her it was time. She was about to find out whether her lack of support would hurt her.

The guard led her up the stairs and into a short hall. Her public defender—whose name, she now knew, was Charles Huett—met her there.

"Remember what I told you," he said. "Guilty or not guilty: that's all the judge wants to know."

Ruth nodded. She breathed deeply and prayed for the strength to be able to speak on her own behalf, since he would not. She had spoken up for Daisy in the grocery store because she'd seen Daisy as worthy of defending. Could she do the same for herself?

Charles led her through a side door into the courtroom. The guard followed, leaving Ruth sandwiched between two men who didn't seem to care about her plight. From what she could see, both of them had already decided she was guilty.

As she entered the courtroom, she kept her head low. She passed by three people who were at desks, then stopped at the table and chairs on the defendant's side of the room. But as she lifted her head to the area behind the railing that was designated for spectators, Ruth froze.

All three rows of chairs were filled, and an additional row stood at the back.

The room was filled with Amish people. *Her* Amish people.

Ruth's heart beat faster, and she nearly cried out to ask why they were all there. Row by row, she took in the sight: Connie, Leah, Frannie, Paul, Bishop Yoder, sweet little Daisy, and even Rachel Miller . . . or rather, Rachel Stolzfus by now, surely? Ruth's heart caught at the thought, but she pushed it away.

Why were they all there, though? This made no sense.

She looked to the rear wall and saw Micah leaning back against it with his arms folded. His longish hair fell forward as he gave her a single nod. The whole scene felt surreal to Ruth. All the Amish people looked out of place in the courtroom, but then again, most people did. Including the few Englischers who were sitting in the seats. Ruth supposed they were there to support the other defendants who would be brought in for their own arraignments. As her gaze passed over them, Ruth found it interesting that she thought of them as Englischers when she no longer thought of herself that way.

Charles tugged on her arm. "Turn around," he whispered harshly. She did as she was told, but not before catching Micah's attention one last time. She knew this was all his doing. How she loved this man. She would love him forever.

"Danki," she mouthed to him and turned to take her place at her table.

"All rise," the guard at the front of the room announced. "The Honorable Judge Michael Evans presiding."

All in the courtroom stood, and a moment later, the judge entered the room. His glasses hung at the tip of his nose, and he wore a black robe with a white collar showing at the top. Once he was seated behind his bench, everyone else took their own seats. Ruth found her chair to be hard and uncomfortable. The court, she observed, didn't make any of this easy.

Someone read the docket number, and before Ruth knew it, the judge was looking from her to the papers in front of him and back again.

"Well, you don't see this too often," he said. "You should know, Ruth"—he looked down at file—"Ruth *Griffin*, that this court is blind to stereotypes. You being Amish will not change the procedure that I hold in my court. Crime is still crime, no matter who perpetrates it. Do you understand?"

Ruth felt her face flush, and the words she wanted to say stuck to her tongue. "I-I understand, but Your Honor—"

"Your Honor," her public defender cut her off. "My client understands the rules of this court and will abide by them."

"Very good, and how does your client plead? Guilty or not guilty?"

Her public defender looked at her and nodded. "Now," he whispered.

Ruth hated not having a voice to speak for her, but it appeared that this wasn't the time for her to finally speak up for herself either.

"N-not guilty," she said, but the words weren't very loud.

The judge leaned in. "I believe that was a not-guilty plea, am I correct?"

Her public defender replied, "Yes, Your Honor. Not guilty."

"Very well. Bail is set for one million dollars. We will reconvene in one month." The judge brought his gavel down with a loud crack that ricocheted through Ruth's body.

One million dollars?

She turned to Charles. "Why so much?" she asked as her body grew numb.

"Because you've shown you're a flight risk. Now be quiet and go back with the guard to your cell."

Ruth looked up at the judge, who was preparing to move on to the next case. "Your Honor, may I please say something in my defense?"

The judge peered up at her over the rim of his glasses. "Mr. Huett, get your client under control and out of my courtroom."

"I'm sorry, Your Honor. Right away." Charles grabbed Ruth's forearm and pulled her up out of her seat. Ruth had no choice but to go. But she couldn't do so without telling her side.

"Please, if you would just listen to me," she implored the judge. "I could tell you how Taylor used me to try to steal money from the bank. He owed someone a lot of money. There's more to his death, and it doesn't have anything to do with me."

Charles pulled her harder toward the exit. The guard came over to help.

"If you hope to make a plea bargain, you'd better keep quiet," her attorney whispered.

"You mean change to guilty?" Ruth stared at him. "But I didn't kill anyone! Why would I do that?"

The judge cut in, "Because it will give you a shorter sentence, Miss Griffin. Don't think for a second that I will simply take your word about the events of that night. The DA wouldn't have brought a case if they didn't have one."

"So my testimony doesn't matter?" Her voice grew louder. No one seemed to care what was happening to her.

"You'll have your day in court," the judge said. "But today is not that day."

Ruth's eyes filled with tears of frustration. She looked to the back of the room and saw Micah staring at one of the Englisch men sitting in the gallery. Ruth wondered what he was looking at.

Then she realized that she, too, recognized the man. But from where?

Micah thought it strange that the man who had been fighting with Taylor Williams at the bar would be attending Ruth's arraignment. He didn't know what to make of this, and most of his attention was still focused on Ruth. He didn't like the way her lawyer was pulling her toward the door as she tried to speak for herself. No one was listening to her. Not even the judge.

Ruth pleaded, "If I could just tell you what Taylor did, you'll see I'm not a criminal. In fact, I made a very clear choice *not* to be one when I wouldn't steal for him."

The judge banged his gavel repeatedly. "Order in my court! If I were you, I would zip those lips."

"Let her speak!" Micah hollered from the back of the room. Paul echoed his words, and one by one, others from his community did the same.

The judge hammered down his gavel even harder. "This is an arraignment! This is not a trial. She can speak at her trial."

"If you won't let her speak, then I'll speak for her." Micah spoke loudly and with conviction. "Ruth Griffin didn't kill anyone. I was there. Taylor Williams was alive when Ruth left. But there was someone else who argued with Taylor that night."

Micah looked toward the man he'd seen in the back row.

But he was gone.

Micah scanned the room and saw him heading out the side door. "Stop that man!" he yelled, and the guard ran at the Englischer and grabbed hold of his arm.

"Let me go! I didn't do anything wrong," the guy yelled. "You can't keep me against my will. I know my rights!"

The judge said, "You will stay right there until I say you may leave." He turned back to Micah. "Are you saying this is the man who argued with Taylor Williams that night?"

"Ja, this is the man. I'll put it in writing. I had forgotten all about the argument until now. The fact that he is here should concern people. He and Taylor nearly came to blows in the game room earlier in the night. Taylor owed him money, and it sounded like it was a lot. I expect the amount he owed matches the amount of money Taylor wanted Ruth to steal for him."

The judge sighed and looked at the man. "What's your name?"

The man shot Micah a searing glare. "Leon Camp," he said to the judge. "But I don't have any idea what this Amish man is talking about. He's lying."

The judge turned to the DA. "I'm assuming you've already spoken to Mr. Camp?"

The DA rifled through his file. "Uh . . . uh . . . um, I don't think I have. And I don't see a report in here from the police either."

Judge Evans sighed and leaned back; a look of anger covered his face. "You've brought a case for murder without a full investigation of possible suspects that were at this bar that night? Are you sure you want to go through with this right now?"

The DA stood, holding the open file in front of him and

flipping through its pages as if the answer would jump out at him. "Your Honor, I . . . I felt Ruth Griffin had probable cause to kill Mr. Williams. He had gotten her fired. It indicated motive."

"Owing a lot of money to someone would indicate motive too. Wouldn't you want to look into that as well?"

The DA sighed and nodded. "Yes, Your Honor." He looked at Leon Camp. "I would appreciate if the police could take him into custody and interview him."

The officer holding Leon nodded and led him from the room.

Just then, Leon Camp broke from the guard's hands and ran for the door again. He made it all the way through but quickly reappeared.

Daed and Elder Joseph were in the doorway behind him.

Micah smiled. "Danki, Daed," he said as the guard handcuffed the man this time.

Daed said, "The Amish protect their own."

Ruth smiled through tears as she stood and ran to the short wall that separated her from them. "Danki, Daed." He approached the wall and enfolded her in his arms.

"Danki," she said again, laying her head on his chest.

"Shh, Dochder, all will be well."

The judge brought down his gavel again. "This has got to be the strangest arraignment I've ever had in my court," he announced. "But as of this moment, it is over. And so is this case. Unless a new, reasonable case is built against you, Ruth Griffin, you're free to go." He banged the gavel again.

The people from Micah's community cheered and rushed to Ruth and Daed. As Micah watched, Mamm took her into her arms. Connie stood beside her, waiting her turn. Then Ruth reached for Connie and wept.

As Micah made his way toward her, an Englisch woman cut him off. At first he didn't recognize her, but when she reached Ruth, he realized it was Kathy.

"I'm here to take you home," he heard Kathy say, and Micah very nearly opened his mouth to speak up for Ruth again. He wanted to tell Kathy that Ruth would be going back with him.

But then he remembered that he would be marrying Rachel when they returned to Lititz. Besides, Ruth had made it clear she didn't love him. Why would she want to return to the Amish?

Micah looked away, and instead of walking over to Ruth, he found Rachel and stood beside her, just as he'd promised Ruth he would do.

CHAPTER TWENTY-ONE

"Take me home?" Ruth struggled to understand what Kathy was saying. "This makes no sense. You made it clear I had no home with you anymore. And honestly, I never did."

"Don't be foolish," Kathy scolded her. She looked around at the crowd of Amish people and seemed almost to shrink away from them. "You must see that I am the only home you have. You've been cleared, so no one will think anything negatively of me or you now. Let's get out of here."

Ruth thought that a tiny, one-room studio would be better than going back to Kathy's house. She looked around the room and saw that Micah and Rachel were sitting together. They were undoubtedly married now. But that didn't mean she still couldn't return and live with Connie.

Bishop Yoder had told her she was always welcome. She searched the room for him now and found him with his kindly wife. They were sitting in the second row, and at their smiles of welcome, Ruth turned back to Kathy.

"Actually, I have a home. It's in Lititz. Thank you, Kathy, for your offer and for your many years of caring for me, but I think it's time I find my own way."

Kathy looked affronted, but said, "Well, if you change your mind, you know where to find me." She turned to leave but stopped. Looking back, she said to Ruth, "I'm glad you're free." The expression on her face was gentler than usual.

Ruth smiled at her choice of words and their double meaning. Kathy knew very well that Ruth had never felt free living with her.

At Ruth's nod, Kathy headed to the double doors at the back and disappeared through them. Ruth frowned as she wondered if that would be the last time she would see her sister. She hoped it wouldn't be.

Ruth turned to Connie and reached for the woman. As soon as Connie felt her touch, she opened her arms to receive Ruth. "I would like to go home with you," Ruth whispered.

Connie sighed and clung to Ruth. "My home is your home, and it will always be open to you, for however long you need it."

When Ruth pulled back, she noticed Micah and Rachel coming down the aisle side by side. Although she felt like someone had kicked her in the stomach, she plastered the biggest smile she could muster up onto her face.

"Ruth, I'm so happy for you," Micah said before she could speak.

She nodded at him and Rachel. "I'm happy for the both of you. Congratulations on your . . . wedding." Her voice cracked.

Rachel said, "We decided to postpone until after . . . this, but danki. That is kind of you."

Ruth sought Micah's gaze. His nod confirmed Rachel's words. "We'll marry when we return. It was more important to make sure you were free."

"I want the same for you," Ruth whispered. Did he understand what she meant by that? "If I in any way discouraged you from having that, I am sorry." It occurred to her that perhaps family wasn't what Micah needed most after all. A family was what Ruth needed most, but she should not have placed that expectation on him, and she felt guilty for having done so.

Micah's big dream was to sing. . . . It had always been to sing.

Micah lifted a hand as if to reach out to her, but he quickly dropped it and made a fist at his side. He pressed his lips together, then said, "Every decision I made, I made alone. But you were right. Family is more important than anything. I have no regrets." He dropped his gaze immediately, and she could tell that his last four words were not the truth. Ruth worried that perhaps it would not be wise after all for her to return to Lititz.

She swallowed hard and was about to ask him if he would be okay with her living with Connie, when Paul came up to her side.

"Ruth, I need to speak with you," he said with a voice full of respect.

"All right."

"I-I am so sorry. Can you ever forgive me for how I treated you?"

Ruth smiled and reached out a hand to touch his forearm. "It's all forgiven and forgotten. If I hope to receive forgiveness for my wrongs, then I must give it as well."

Paul sighed and smiled. Then he turned to Rachel. "Look, I know I'm not as good-looking as my Bruder, but if you would have me, Rachel, I would really like to marry you."

All around them, people gasped again. Ruth looked to Micah to see what he thought of his brother stepping in and taking his bride. Would he take this as a blessing or not? Had Paul truly just freed him to go live the life he really wanted? *Paul?* The very brother who had long demanded that Micah do what was expected of him and get married?

Tears blurred Ruth's eyes as realization took root. Micah was free. Free to sing, free to pursue the life he had long wanted.

That is, if Rachel accepted Paul's proposal.

The room fell silent, and all eyes turned to Rachel.

Rachel tilted her head and looked at Paul. "I think you're the humblest person I've ever met. And the kindest." Her eyes sparkled. "And I'll have to admit, you seem very good-looking to me." A gentle smile cracked her lips, and her face flushed to a pretty pink. "I would be honored to marry you, Paul Stolzfus."

"But I thought you all wanted—" Micah started, but his mother cut him off.

"What we want is for all of our children to be happy," Leah said matter-of-factly. She clapped her hands. "I think this is wunderbaar! After meeting sweet Rachel, I do feel that she and Paul would be much better suited for each other. Someday you'll see that it was for the best." She nodded at her oldest son, silently urging him to agree with her. Leah was giving Micah no choice, and Ruth appreciated what she was doing for him. Just as Paul had done for his brother, Leah Stolzfus was setting her son free.

"I suppose you're right." Micah took Rachel's hand. "I hope we can be friends, especially since we will be family. And just so you know, there are no hard feelings for you turning me down for a second time." He grinned. "I know you will be happy with my Bruder. He is a *gut* man."

Rachel nodded and turned back to Paul. It was clear now that she was smitten with him and happy with the turn of events.

"And I want you two to have the farm," Micah told his brother.

Paul stood stunned, and as people in the courtroom congratulated the newly engaged couple, Ruth was left standing alone with Micah. She had only one thing to say to him. If she didn't speak her heart, she would regret it forever.

She leaned close and whispered, "Chase your dreams, Micah. Don't ever give up."

Micah shook his head. "I was wrong, and you showed me that. I only have one dream worth chasing, Ruth, and I'm looking at her right now." Micah's words stunned her to silence. She stood stock-still, feeling all eyes behind her on her back. "You told the policeman you don't love me," he said, "but you can rest assured that I will never stop trying to make myself worthy of your love. So go ahead, leave if you want to. But this will not be the last time you see me. When you need someone to talk to, I will be there. When you need a friend, a helping hand, or a comforting song, I will be there. And someday, when you decide you want to belong somewhere, I will do everything in my power to convince you that you belong with me."

Slowly, Ruth turned to face him. She had done everything possible to disguise her feelings for Micah so that he would never have to choose between her and his family, or even between her and his music. But by the sound of it, he'd already made his choice.

And what he'd chosen was her.

Ruth's silence terrified Micah. The whole courtroom was watching and waiting for her response, but none of them stood to lose what he did.

She looked at his parents, then back at him. Under her breath, she asked, "What about your music?"

There was no sense in denying his love of singing to anyone anymore. They all knew anyway.

Micah held his head high and said, "My whole life, I have wanted to sing so that I could affect lives in a positive way. But it wasn't until you came into my life that I saw what affecting people positively really looked like. I saw how you were able to affect others, and I also saw how my music affected you. I've watched you transform from a shy and lonely girl to a strong and sure woman. I loved singing for you, but that singing was never about me. It was about allowing my songs to connect you to Gött. I understand now. I can't help people by becoming famous. Gött is the only one who should be famous. And when I sing, it will be to bring Him glory only."

"That's beautiful, Micah," Ruth whispered. She chewed on her lower lip. She seemed undecided about what to do or say next. His words may have touched her, but that didn't mean that she loved him.

"What else can I say to you to prove my love to you is forever? What can I do to earn your love?"

She scanned the room and appeared to look directly at someone. Micah followed her gaze and saw Bishop Yoder nod at her. When Ruth looked back at him, Micah was unsure of what had just transpired between her and the church elder.

"There's something you need to know." Ruth held her head high now.

"Ja?" Worry filled him. Was his Lieb in trouble?

"Micah, I'm returning to Lititz to be Amish, and I will never leave again. I would never ask you to close that door on your dreams, knowing . . ." She swallowed hard. "Well, knowing how you feel . . ." She glanced around and whispered, "About your music."

Micah let a sigh of relief escape his lungs. Had he not made himself clear enough to her? He smiled, first tentatively, then so full that his lips nearly cracked. "Ach, Ruth, I thought you were hurt or sick or something." He reached for both her hands and brought them to his lips, kissing each one. "This makes me so happy. Happier than I have ever been."

"Really?" Her hopeful expression endeared her to him even more.

He nodded. "I intend to marry you, Ruth Griffin." He tilted his head as tears built behind his eyes. "Whether that happens this week or this year is up to you. But you are the only one for me, and I'm not going anywhere. Where you are will be where I am for always and forever. Do you understand now?"

Ruth's eyes widened and shimmered with unshed tears. She looked to her right where his mother was standing just behind Daisy. "Mamm," Ruth asked with trembling lips, "I would like to marry your son, if that's all right with you. But you should know," she continued gently, "that I will always encourage Micah to sing. Our home will always be filled with music. I won't try to change him."

Leah sighed, and tears filled her eyes. "I had hoped you would want to, but after the way I treated you, I didn't dare ask."

"You only did what you thought best because you love him," Ruth said gently. "I could never fault you for that. And I want you to know that I love him too." She looked back at him and captured his full attention. "I love him so much."

"You do?" Micah asked, unable to believe his ears.

She nodded. "With all my heart."

"And you want to marry me?" Micah's voice caught. He was afraid he was imagining all of this.

"I would marry you right now, if I could." She smiled.

Bishop Yoder stood up and said loudly, "I think I can handle that."

People in the crowd whispered their confusion, then Daed said, "But she has not been baptized. How can a wedding take place?"

Bishop Yoder looked at his wife and then at Connie. Both women wore huge smiles. "Several days ago, Ruth came to me and asked to join our community. She made the decision to be baptized with my Fraa and Connie as her witnesses. I assure you, Ruth is able to marry Micah right now, if she so wishes."

Daisy shouted, "Wait just a second! Ruth is already Amish?"

Bishop Yoder smiled. "That she is, child."

"Wunderbaar!" Daisy exclaimed and clapped once, and everyone laughed.

Just then the judge spoke up. He'd been watching the scene unfold along with everyone else, and Micah had completely forgotten that he was still there. "If you're fixing to get married, I can also take care of that right now."

Bishop Yoder gave a nod of approval. "That would be uncustomary, but so is this whole thing. I would be willing to make it a double ceremony. Paul, Rachel, what say you?"

"Ach, ja!" Paul shouted. He reached for Rachel's hand and led her forward. "But Micah, the house is yours. I would like to build on the back property and work the land with you, like we always have, if you're willing?"

Micah looked to Ruth, and at her exuberant nod, Micah agreed, and they joined his brother and Rachel at the bench. And right there in the courthouse, the Stolzfus family grew in numbers and in love.

After the vows were over and everyone had been congratulated, Elder Joseph walked up to Micah and Ruth.

"You have been hiding a strong voice?" he asked Micah. "I would like to hear it, and perhaps you would consider becoming the new *Vorsinger* in the church."

Ruth tilted her head. "What's that?"

Elder Joseph replied, "The person who leads the church community in making worshipful music."

"He'll take the job!" Ruth said quickly. "When can he start?"

Micah smiled. "She knows me well." He laughed. "Ja, I would love to lead the music. Danki for considering me." He looked at his wife. "And danki for loving me just the way I am. None of this would have been possible if it weren't for you."

"There will be no more secret melodies in our house." Ruth laid her head on his chest.

Micah sighed and pulled her close. They would be heading

back to Lititz very soon. But wherever they were, as long as Ruth was in his arms, he was already home.

Micah began to hum the tune that he knew Ruth loved so much. She lifted her face to his as he sang the words, but this time she joined him. Her melodic voice melded perfectly with his, and the song had never sounded more powerful. As they finished the final verse, Ruth stood up on her tiptoes and kissed him on the lips in front of everyone. When the people around them giggled and gasped, she pulled away and said, "Did I just do something wrong . . . again?"

"Nee, let them watch," Micah said, and he leaned down and kissed his Fraa thoroughly, setting the stage for the marriage of a lifetime.

Up to this point, we've been doing all the writing. Now it's *your* turn!

Tell us what you think about this book, the characters, the town, or anything else you'd like to share with us about this series. We can't wait to hear from *you*!

Log on to give us your feedback at:
https://www.surveymonkey.com/r/LancasterRomance

Annie's® FICTION